THE STRONGEST SHAPE

Tessa Cárdenas

Dreamspinner Press

Published by
Dreamspinner Press
4760 Preston Road
Suite 244-149
Frisco, TX 75034
http://www.dreamspinnerpress.com/

The Strongest Shape

Cover Art by Paul Richmond   http://www.paulrichmondstudio.com
Cover Design by Mara McKennen

ISBN: 978-1-61581-235-6

Printed in the United States of America
First Edition
November, 2009

eBook edition available
eBook ISBN: 978-1-61581-236-3

Dedicated to Jessie and Samantha.
Jessie, for being my other half.
Samantha, for being my muse
and the reason I started writing again.

Special thanks to Kelly, Karen, Jocelyn, and Wendy
for all the help editing so that I could tell my story.

CHAPTER 1

CALEB doesn't actually remember how he ended up coming home with Jason. He remembers going to Jason's concert alone after Damian broke up with him. He remembers ordering the first few shots of vodka. He even remembers telling Jason that his music was inspiring. He just has no idea how he reached the point of waking up in Jason's apartment. It's not like he's ever spoken more than a few words to the guy. He's hoping there wasn't a hook up involved because it must have been pathetic if he ended up by himself on the couch.

"Coffee, water, or aspirin?" Jason looks at him through the window of the kitchen when he notices that Caleb's awake.

"All three?"

Jason laughs, but he nods before bringing everything to the living room.

"So last night…." Caleb bites his lip. He's really going to have to pay Jason back if he promised Jason something and then passed out on the couch.

"Nothing happened. You did offer, but I have a girlfriend."

Shit. He's lucky Jason didn't kick his ass. "Sorry."

"It's okay. Unless this Damian guy is going to change his mind and try to kick my ass for taking you home." Jason's smiling, but he still looks a little worried.

"He's really not." Damian has probably already moved on to someone else. Caleb takes a sip of his coffee to buy time. "So if you're straight, why did you take me home?"

"The bar was closing, and you wouldn't tell the bartender where you lived so she could call a cab. I was still loading up." Jason shrugs. "It was me or the cops."

"Thanks." He really owes Jason something. Maybe he can buy an entire box of CDs and send them to everyone he knows. Either way, he should probably clear out. "I'll just call a cab."

"You have money for a cab?" Jason asks.

When Caleb checks his wallet, he only finds three dollars and a phone number he doesn't recognize.

"Don't worry about it," Jason says before Caleb can start thinking about how the hell he's getting home. "A friend of mine's coming by to pick something up. I can drive you after that if you don't mind hanging out for a while."

"Thanks. I can pay you back for gas or something." Hell, he's not even sure where Jason lives. He could be miles away from his apartment. He might not even be in LA anymore.

"No big deal." Jason sits in the recliner next to the couch and flips on the TV.

"So either you owe me for something I don't remember, or I redefined pathetic." This is why Caleb likes to drink at home where the worst he can do is call and ramble to people who are already used to him. At least his friends will tell him that they never liked Damian, and he deserves better and all that other stuff people say when your boyfriend leaves you.

"Do you really wanna know?"

2

He's sure he doesn't, but he has to decide if he can ever go to one of Jason's shows again.

"Yeah."

"You told me you couldn't go home because Damian was packing up his stuff. You moved out here from New York because he's an actor on some new show. Now he thinks he's too good for you and he's moving in with some other guy you don't know."

Caleb groans. Damian is probably going to kill him after this shows up in the tabloids. It's not that he still cares if he ruined Damian's career. "He's really not that famous yet."

"Don't worry. If I sold that kind of stuff to the paparazzi, I have other friends who'd be after me. They're already gonna give me shit for talking to a photographer without a job in this city."

"I'm a fashion photographer. I don't do that climbing over fences and chasing down cars shit."

"I promise you told me that a few times last night. You don't have to run back to New York, though. You can freelance in town if you know the right people."

Caleb shrugs and looks away. He knows that. The problem is that the right people he knows also know Damian.

"I know people too. I can introduce you," Jason says before shrugging and admitting, "Actually my friend Chris knows people. He's out of town right now, but when he gets back, he can help you out."

"Why?" He's starting to wonder if Jason's really straight. He doesn't want to go crawling back to New York because he can't survive in LA without Damian, but he doesn't want to be sucking Jason's dick for jobs either. He'll go back to New York before he lowers himself to that.

"I came out here by myself. I probably would've gone running back to Iowa if a couple people hadn't helped me out." Jason gives him a smile, getting up as the front door opens and closes.

The man Jason comes back with is someone Caleb's seen at a few of Jason's shows. His blonde hair falls just above his shoulders. It's loose and wavy. Caleb can't help wondering how it would feel to run his fingers through it. He's not Damian, but Damian's hair was always sticky with gel anyway.

"You switched teams without mentioning it?" The new guy asks when he sees Caleb.

"No. Just gave him a couch for the night." Jason nods to him. "Caleb, this is Scott."

"Actor?" Scott looks him over, and he's not sure if it's because he looks like shit or because Scott's interested. If he's lucky, it's the latter and Caleb will have a chance to find out.

"Photographer."

Scott gives Jason a look, but Jason just rolls his eyes. "He does fashion spreads and that fancy stuff. It's not like any of us are getting followed around like Britney. You wish someone besides Chris cared enough to take your picture."

Scott shrugs before bending down to pick up a couple of cords Jason had left on the floor. "Maybe we should've tried a little harder to make it to your show."

"So you could look at him wrong and cause a scene?"

"Just trying to figure out how your night ended up with him on your couch." Scott nods in Caleb's direction. "If he's on my way, I can give him a ride home."

When Jason shrugs, Scott groans before Caleb can interrupt with his address. "You brought him home and you don't even know him? This isn't Nebraska. He could've stolen everything in your apartment. Chris is going to explode."

4

"Chris didn't know me when he invited me over," Jason says.

"Chris invited you to a party, and you didn't spend the night. He liked your music, and he needed a new project."

"Caleb didn't steal anything anyway."

"I guess that's something." Scott sighs and turns to look at Caleb again. "So where are you going?"

Caleb throws out the address to his apartment, and Scott nods. "It's not that out of my way. Come on."

The first few minutes in the car are silent until Scott taps his leg to get his attention away from the window. "It's nothing against you. Jason's just a little too trusting in this town."

"It's cool." Hell, he's lucky Jason didn't do anything to *him*. He's the one who got so drunk that he let some guy he didn't know take him home.

When Scott stops in front of his apartment building, Damian's car is gone.

"Something in there you're scared of?" Scott asks when Caleb doesn't move.

"No. Sorry." Caleb starts to open the door, but Scott catches his wrist.

"Why didn't you have anyone to take you home last night except Jason?"

"I went to the show by myself." He doesn't add that Damian was supposed to go with him.

"And got really drunk by yourself knowing that you didn't have a ride home?" When Caleb doesn't give him a real answer, Scott tries something else. "Where are you from?"

"Dallas, but I lived in New York for about four years. I'll be all right. I don't usually get drunk and let random guys take me home."

5

"Chris was born in Dallas. Ended up moving to Oklahoma though."

"Yeah?" Caleb says before he can stop himself. He hasn't met a lot of people from Texas since he left, and it would be nice to talk about the Rangers without having to explain he doesn't mean hockey.

"Yeah. He's out of town for a couple weeks. He got some gigs by himself up north, but I'll introduce you when he gets back."

"You don't have to make me your new project." It's probably an asshole thing to say, but it's not like he just stumbled off the farm. The more he thinks about it, the more he thinks of people he might be able to call who never really liked working with Damian that much. Of course, that's just gonna get him a job, not anything else. All his friends in LA are Damian's friends.

"You came over here by yourself?" Scott asks.

"No."

"You came over here with whoever's not in that apartment anymore?" When Caleb doesn't answer, Scott pulls out a piece of paper. "Write down your number. We'll call you."

"Why?"

"Well, you didn't end up stealing anything from Jason, did you?"

☙☾

"JASON'S having some people over. You should come," Scott says when he calls a week later.

"Then why isn't Jason calling?"

"His girl's visiting from Idaho. He's always distracted the first few days," Scott says. Caleb's pretty sure Jason said he was from Iowa, but he was kind of hung over at the time. "So just show up. Bring some beer if it makes you feel better."

Any doubts Caleb had vanish when Jason opens the door on Friday. He smiles and takes the six-pack of beer out of Caleb's hands as he pulls him inside.

"Come on in and meet everyone."

"Hey. You showed up," Scott says.

"I didn't really have anything else," Caleb answers before he realizes how pathetic that sounds.

"We're glad you came. My friend Danielle wants to meet you."

Scott takes his arm and leads him past Jason into the living room. Danielle's got the kind of red hair he's seen a lot of models try to get with dye, and even sitting he can tell she's tall enough that she'd only need a pair of heels to look him in the eye. He'd thought Scott invited him so he wouldn't be the only single one at the party—though he's not sure if Scott wanted a date or a wingman. Now he's not sure if Scott's after Danielle. Caleb needs to ask Jason if he told any of these people that he's gay.

"Scott, seriously, you need to be more specific when you tell me you invited some new guy Jason met," Danielle says before Scott even introduces him. Great. He probably made an ass of himself at the club. Caleb opens his mouth to apologize, but Danielle waves it off. "Don't worry. I heard the story, but we left before Jason found you at the bar. I just remember noticing you at the show."

"Is he your ex or something?" Scott asks.

"No, silly. He's Caleb Moss. He took the pictures when I did that spread for *TeenChic*," Danielle says. Caleb really wishes he could remember what shoot she's talking about, but most of the

7

models he notices are guys. It must've only been one shoot, because he likes to think he would have at least a vague memory of a girl he'd worked with over and over.

"It's okay. It was two years ago, and I'm more into acting now. Or I'm trying to be. It's not working out so well. I'm mostly playing 'high school student number three' right now."

"But she's a very hot 'high school student number three'," Scott says, leaning over to kiss her forehead.

"So is it way too early to ask you to do new headshots for me even though I probably can't actually afford you?" Danielle asks. "You just made me look so good last time. The headshots I have now are okay, but you could do better. Then maybe I'll actually get a job."

"Sure," Caleb says even though he's not sure that Jason didn't put her up to asking.

"Awesome," Danielle pulls him down on the couch next to her as Jason comes back to hand him a beer. "I like him. I vote we keep him."

ℰℭℛ

"GLAD you came?" Scott's alone on the balcony, plunking out a melody on his guitar.

"Yeah. Thanks." Caleb takes the chair across from Scott and watches him play a while. He's past the funny stage of drunk and onto the sleepy part. He should call a cab soon.

"Like it? There's no lyrics yet."

"Yeah. It's good."

"You play?" Scott asks.

8

"A little. Not like you." He used to play for Damian, but Damian didn't notice how much he messed up. Scott's on a whole other level.

"Let me hear." Scott tries to pass him the guitar, but he doesn't take it.

"Man, I'm drunk. I'm not that great when I'm sober."

"So we'll blame it on the beer if you mess up." Scott puts the guitar in his hands.

Caleb's also going to blame the beer for the way he doesn't realize he's singing along to the music until Scott says, "Well, how about that. You've got a voice too."

"It's nothing." Caleb hands him back the guitar, hoping it's too dark for Scott to notice he's blushing. "I should get going. I remembered cab fare this time."

"Jason's not gonna care if you crash here. Most of us are."

"Maybe next time." Jason might not care, but he'd like to prove he can handle himself and get home on his own.

"Sure. I've got a show tomorrow if you can make it. I've got a bet with Jason that you'll like me better."

CHAPTER 2

IT'S three more weeks before Caleb finally meets Chris. With everyone talking about him; no one mentioned how hot he was. His hair is only a few inches shorter than Scott's, but instead of blond and wavy, it's straight and light brown. Scott just says, "Hey, this is Chris," like that's enough of an explanation all on its own. Maybe it is enough because in the last three weeks, Caleb's already heard about ten different opinions of Chris, and half of the group seems to think Chris might hate him on the spot.

Chris smiles, cocks his head and says, "Heard you can play."

"I'm all right," Caleb answers, wondering when Scott was talking about him and how he can get out of playing for Chris. Scott and Chris are real musicians. They both have their own albums and they've recorded a few together, while he just plays around sometimes to get the edge off. Two weeks ago, it took a six pack of Corona before Scott convinced Caleb to pick up a guitar, but Chris doesn't let him get through ten minutes. Caleb wants to say no, but Chris takes his beer bottle right out of his hand and replaces it with a guitar.

"I don't really play much," he says, trying to hand the guitar back, but Chris leans back on the couch and refuses to return his drink until he plays a song.

He plays just enough to get his beer, but Chris smirks. "Not bad."

"You were doubting me?" Scott elbows Chris and takes the guitar.

"You shouldn't start a story with 'well, I was kinda wasted at the time', if you want me to trust your judgment. Remember that time in Nashville when you were doing body shots?"

Scott shoots him a look, and Chris raises an eyebrow, but he shrugs and changes the subject before Caleb can ask what the hell they're talking about.

"I saw Danielle's headshots. They're good. Better than what I did for her."

Caleb glares at Scott. Someone should have told him the pictures he was replacing were taken by *Chris*. No wonder everyone thought Chris would hate him right away.

"It's all right. Just a hobby. I'd have gotten onto her if she passed up the chance to get you to do them," Chris says before he can come up with some kind of pathetic apology. "Looked up some of your stuff myself. It's good. Got anything new going on?"

"Yeah. I called my friend Dan. He's trying to get me some ad campaigns. That kind of thing."

"As long as you're not crossing over to the dark side."

"I have standards," Caleb says, taking another long drink of his beer. "And I don't need to piss anyone off who I might want to work with later."

"Yeah." Chris tries not to be obvious about catching Scott's eye and shrugging. Caleb hopes that shrug means he passed whatever test Chris was giving.

Caleb nods to the guitar Chris already set aside. "So when do I get to hear you play?"

"You wanna hear anything special?" Chris asks. When Caleb shakes his head, Chris just starts strumming.

"Just don't flatter him too much. He doesn't need it. His head is big enough already." Scott elbows him in the side and smiles. Chris glances away from the guitar to look at them, but he just continues with the song without commenting.

℘℅

THERE'S no single thing that makes him suspicious. Caleb doesn't catch them sneaking a kiss or find an incriminating picture. He can explain the way they finish each other's sentences by reminding himself that they've been writing music together for years. He can tell himself that Chris is always at Scott's because Chris can't cook for shit and Scott always has something on the stove. Hell, that's why *he's* always at Scott's.

But the more time he spends with them, the more he notices the looks they throw each other and the innuendos Chris slips into conversation like he's trying to make a point. It's enough that Caleb starts watching, making note of how many ways Chris finds to touch Scott, whether he's just brushing a hand over Scott's back as he passes or the way his fingers comb through Scott's hair when he makes fun of them both for being blonde.

He doesn't do anything about it until he notices things are changing. Chris's lips tighten when Caleb shows up at Scott's. He stops hassling Caleb about playing, stops saying that now he wants to hear that voice he heard about, or making fun of Caleb because they both manage to look hot with longer hair, while he looks like someone used a chili bowl to cut his hair in the picture they found in his high school yearbook.

Caleb decides he should give them some space. They never do anything around him so he figures if he's right, Chris is probably sick of waiting for him to leave so they can fuck. Maybe if he backs off, Chris will like him again.

The problem is that half the time, Scott invites him over, so he has to make up excuses. He tells Scott he's in talks with a few designers about shooting spreads of their fall lines even though he hates meetings. He'd make all his deals by e-mail if he could. After that, it only makes sense to say he's working out the contracts. He thinks about calling Jason, but he's always hanging out with Chris and Scott, so he ignores Jason's call when Jason finally notices he's gone missing. He goes on a mission to find the best Chinese food in LA and orders from a different restaurant every night for two weeks.

He's expecting his latest test sample when he finds Chris at the door instead.

"You got a job? Must be happening soon with you networking every fucking day." Chris doesn't ask if he can come in. He just pushes past Caleb and wanders into the kitchen where his eyes follow the collection of takeout boxes. "You break up with a girl you forgot to mention?"

"No."

"You're not really working. I know I don't get paid thousands to shoot stick figures in ugly clothes like you do, but I take side jobs often enough. You're Caleb Moss. It doesn't take this much for you to get a job." Chris sniffs one of the containers and starts tossing things into a trash bag Caleb didn't know he had. It's not a question.

"No."

"You figured out about me and Scott?" This one *is* a question. Chris doesn't look at him when he asks, just keeps tossing out any trash he can find.

"Yeah."

"Guess I don't have to ask what you think about it."

"What? You think I give a shit?" That answers how much Jason let slip about the night he took Caleb home. For whatever reason, he didn't tell Chris about Caleb being gay.

"You've been dodging Scott for a week." There's an edge in his voice, and it's not fair. Caleb's not the one who started answering everything with a grunt two weeks earlier.

"And *now* that's not what you want?"

Chris looks up and stares at him for a second. "How long have you known?"

"Couple months?" Caleb answers. The last thing he expects is for Chris to start laughing.

"You knew? All this time?"

"I was pretty sure." Caleb shrugs. It would help if Chris would let him in on the joke.

Chris laughs until the corners of his eyes are wet, shaking his head as he drops the bag of garbage. "Fuck, I just wanted Scott to tell you."

෨෬

THINGS change a little each day after that. At first it's the same. They hang out, play a few songs, and go through cases of Corona until Chris talks him into singing. Chris gets him on video promising to sing backup vocals on Scott's CD, and he doesn't care that Caleb is too drunk to remember it the next day.

The first time he sees them kiss, Caleb's sitting on the couch with Scott, watching some documentary on Animal Planet. Chris is leaving to meet an actress who wants some headshots—because some people really do have to meet people for jobs—and he leans down to kiss Scott goodbye. It's quick, routine in a way that only comes from years of doing it, and he's already out the door before Scott catches Caleb's eye and realizes they've never kissed in front of him before.

Caleb smiles and shrugs, turns back to the TV, and tries to pretend he's not jealous. He spends the rest of the documentary trying to figure out who and what he's jealous of.

Caleb's not any closer to figuring it out three weeks later, even though Chris and Scott have taken to kissing in front of him more. Not that he sits around and watches them make out, but they seem to give up censoring. He's at Jason's after one of Scott's shows and Chris has Scott pushed up against the wall, his hands tangled in Scott's hair as he talks. Caleb can't hear anything he's saying, but he can get an idea from the way Scott sighs and pushes against him.

So maybe sometimes he does watch them make out. It's hard not to when they're right in front of him.

"Don't let Chris catch you looking at them like that." Danielle's smirking at him when he jerks his head away.

"I wasn't."

"You were, but I won't tell," Danielle sighs. "You know, you should talk to other people when we go out. I know Chris is weird about new people, but he's just paranoid. He got used to you. He'll get used to it if you meet someone."

"Maybe I don't want to meet someone." He should. Damian's been gone a long time. Caleb hasn't even thought of watching his show since it started airing, but it must be doing well because he's seen Damian on two magazine covers.

"Hon, even Chris thinks you have a thing for Scott. Why he hasn't done anything about it none of us can figure out. I'm not sure *Chris* can figure it out, but you shouldn't push your luck. He's not gonna let you have him."

"I don't want to take Scott from him." He really doesn't. That's what *he* can't figure out.

15

"Good." Danielle wraps her arm around his waist and leads him back to where Jason is setting up a game of king's cup.

Two hours later Caleb's trying to sleep on the couch because he's too drunk to go home. He doesn't even try not to hear the soft moans from guest bedroom.

CHAPTER 3

"HE'S still got his own place, you know. If you want to see him, go over there," Scott snaps when Caleb comes over and asks where Chris is.

"Whoa. That's really not what I meant. It was just a question." Caleb thinks he should probably not point out that this is the first time Chris hasn't been at Scott's since he got back into town. It was a fair question.

"Sorry," Scott mumbles, turning back to the couch and sitting down with his guitar. Caleb sits next to him while he plucks out a melody. Scott starts to write it down, then sighs, and erases everything.

"You wanna talk about it?" Caleb asks even though he's never been so great at talking. Scott's a talker though and Caleb's okay with listening.

"We had a fight."

"I figured as much."

"He says I don't write songs for both of us anymore."

"Do you?" He always thought it was confusing how sometimes they'd play together and sometimes they'd play alone, but after a while he'd figured out why. They had different songs when they played alone. The only thing was that Scott signed a lot more solo shows than Chris did, and Scott had added a lot more songs to his solo act.

"Yes! Fuck, now you're taking his side?"

"Hey." Caleb rests his hand on Scott's arm to stop him from getting up. "I'm not taking sides. I'm just asking. I've seen you play together three times and it's always the same songs. I've seen you play yourself four times and you've added two new songs."

"But it's not me. I can't write for both of us when he's not here, and he was gone for three weeks. I just... I need him around longer to get back into it." Scott sighs, setting his guitar aside. "And I need him helping me. I'm sitting here trying to write a song to make him happy, but it doesn't work because I need his help to do it."

"Okay. Did you try telling him that?"

"It turned into a fight about how he's been busy with all his side projects."

"I thought you were going to talk to him about that last week?"

"I might've put it off." Scott bites his lip and picks at his nails instead of looking at Caleb.

"Until you brought it up because you were mad?"

"Maybe."

"You know he's probably sitting at his apartment just as miserable as you are, but he's too damn stubborn to call you. You should just call him, say all this shit without getting mad and he'll come back."

"It's not that simple."

"Because it's actually more complicated or because you're being as stubborn as he is?"

Scott chuckled, finally smiling as he pushes Caleb away from him. "Where were you all those other times we fought?"

"In New York."

"Fine. I'll call him. If next time you promise to go bug him, and make him call me."

"I'll give it a shot."

ℰⱷ

"*YOU* need to catch up," Chris says as he presses Caleb against the back of the couch, straddling his hips and pushing the bottle of tequila to his lips. Maybe this is what they do to everyone who shows up late for what they consider a party, but he's not sure they can call it a party with just him. He's waiting for Scott to say something about his boyfriend sitting in Caleb's lap, but Scott just laughs and holds his hands down while Chris pours tequila down his throat. He takes as much as he can before he chokes, and tequila dribbles down his chin as Chris pulls the bottle back.

"Boy can swallow." Chris laughs and wipes the alcohol off Caleb's chin with his thumb before climbing off and falling on the couch next to him. They started without him, and he's not sure he wants to know how much liquor they went through before he got there to make them this drunk. Scott takes the bottle and puts it to Caleb's lips again, but at least he lets Caleb take it and tip it back himself.

Caleb laughs, letting his head lull against the back of the couch as the alcohol hits his system and fuzzes the world around him. Everything is moving faster than he can process, and when he turns his head back to Chris, Scott has claimed his place in Chris's lap.

They've kissed in front of him a million times now but not like this. Chris pushes his hands under Scott's shirt and claws at his back as Scott attacks his mouth. Scott whines just a little when Chris pushes him away so he can pull Scott's T-shirt over his head, and as soon as it's out of the way, he presses close again, mouthing down Chris's neck.

Caleb wonders if he should leave or at least look away, but if he wanted Caleb to leave, Chris shouldn't have poured tequila down his throat. Caleb's not sure he could walk if he wanted to, and besides, he *really* doesn't want to. His eyes follow Chris's hands as they travel down Scott's back, stopping to clench Scott's ass and pull him closer. Scott's lips break away from his neck with a moan, and he pants as they grind against each other. His fingers fumble with the buttons on Chris's shirt, and his eyes inch open, locking with Caleb's.

Caleb freezes. He should leave. If he's going to leave, he really needs to leave now—except Scott doesn't tell him to leave. Instead, Scott holds his gaze as he strips Chris of his shirt.

Chris opens his eyes then and follows Scott's line of sight. Shit. Scott might be willing to share, but he's seen the way Chris can be. Hell, he's not sure how everyone doesn't know they're fucking just from the way Chris's body language screams *mine*.

Caleb tries to get up, even though he has no idea where he's going to hide. He can't drive, and he'd really rather not spend the night in the bathroom. It doesn't matter anyway, because Chris catches his wrist and holds on; then he turns back to face Scott so their eyes meet. Something is said in that look, but Caleb doesn't know the language. He just knows that Scott nods, and the grip on his hand tightens as Chris fumbles with the button of Scott's jeans.

Caleb relaxes against the couch again, watching as Chris reaches his hand into Scott's jeans and pulls out his cock. Caleb's hard—his cock is pushing against the zipper of his jeans, but he resists the urge to jack off. He's still not sure what his place is in this whole thing, and he sure as hell doesn't want to fuck up and get kicked out.

Scott pushes into Chris's hand, moaning and sucking on Chris's neck as his hands pull open Chris's jeans. When Scott reaches inside, Chris grunts and bucks into Scott's hand, cursing under his breath. They kiss open-mouthed and sloppy until Scott breaks away.

"Fuck me," Scott says, and Chris pulls back, eyes darting to Caleb like he's not sure how much of Scott he wants to share.

"Wanna feel you. Come on. Fuck me. Let him watch. You want him to watch." Scott's voice is low, but Caleb can still catch his words.

Scott whines when Chris grips his hips and pushes him away, but Chris just laughs and pushes harder. "I can't fuck you if I can't get your pants off."

Chris keeps his hands on Scott's waist as Scott stands and shucks off his jeans, barely waiting for Chris to toss aside his own jeans before climbing back into his lap.

"Pushy bottom," Chris mutters under his breath.

"You love it," Scott answers as his lips latch onto Chris's neck.

Chris rolls his eyes in Caleb's direction even though Caleb's pretty sure he *does* love it. His eyes run over Caleb's body and settle where Caleb's cock is pressing against his jeans.

"If you'd rather be alone to jack off, you're kind of missing the point."

He hates being put on the spot, and Chris knows that. Not that Chris has ever given a damn, and he actually thought he was getting used to that. He must not be though, because instead of just giving into what Chris wants, he freezes.

"Fuck it. He's going to make me wait until you start, so hurry the fuck up," Scott bitches, pushing against Chris. Caleb can't help laughing as he unzips his jeans. He never pictured Scott like this in bed, and he's spent enough time thinking about them.

Chris digs in the couch cushions and comes up with lube and a condom, making Caleb moan when he thinks about how much they must have fucked on the couch he always crashes on. He watches as Chris slicks up his fingers and reaches back to press inside, making Scott shudder and push back against him.

Chris fucks Scott open with his fingers, taking his time no matter how much Scott fights him. And Scott sure as hell fights him, fucking himself on Chris's fingers and writhing whenever Chris hits the right spot. Scott takes the condom without asking and rolls it over Chris's cock, slicking him up and stroking until Chris curses and knocks his hand away.

Chris pulls his fingers away from Scott's ass, and his eyes roll back as Scott presses down. They fuck hard and fast, Chris pulling on Scott's cock until he spills over Chris's stomach and falls forward. Caleb moans, and Chris meets his eyes over Scott's shoulder, fucking into Scott's lax body as Caleb jacks himself harder. He wants to reach out, touch Scott, but he doesn't dare.

Chris lets his fingers trail over the come splattered on his stomach before reaching out and pressing his fingers against Caleb's lips. Without thinking about it, Caleb licks the bitter come off Chris's fingers and sucks them into his mouth as he comes.

"So fucking hot," Chris whispers, clutching Scott's ass with his other hand and coming hard.

They sit in silence for a moment before Chris pulls his hand away from Caleb and rubs over Scott's back.

"Gotta get up, babe. Can't pass out on the couch," Chris murmurs to Scott, soft and gentle in a way Caleb's never heard. Suddenly, he feels out of place. Everything else felt like no big deal. But this? This is too intimate, and he's not sure he should see it. He lets his eyes shift away as Scott whines and pulls off, and he doesn't watch as they stumble to their room.

When the sun wakes him at dawn, his head is pounding, and his body aches. He hates the sun in the morning. At his apartment, he has thick curtains over the window so he can sleep late. Today it's okay, though, because Chris and Scott aren't awake yet. Caleb pulls on his clothes and sneaks out the door before he has to suffer through an awkward morning.

CHAPTER 4

SCOTT sends him a text the day after. *We'll call. Just give us some time.* Then there's nothing. No texts, no calls. Just nothing, and Caleb's pretty sure he's not supposed to make the next move.

This time, Caleb decides to find the best pizza in LA. He actually does get a few calls for jobs, but he doesn't feel like returning the messages. Jason calls after a week, wanting to know why he missed Scott's last show, and he makes up some excuse about a shoot that he knows Jason doesn't buy. He doesn't say that the only way he heard about it was the e-mail that went out to everyone or that he waited at home that night, hoping they'd call and actually invite him. Jason doesn't press for answers, but maybe he knows something's up because he mentions that Caleb should call him if he wants to get together. He says they can hang out and play some music without Chris and Scott showing them both up, but Caleb never makes plans. If he gives Jason a chance, Jason will pry something out of him.

He's on the thirteenth pizza place in the phonebook when Chris calls, and he stares at the display for a few seconds before he picks up.

"Hey." It's awkward already. What the hell is he supposed to say? He's sorry he watched them fuck? Because he's really not.

"Hey. Can you come over to Scott's? We'd come to you, but I don't want to have to clean up two weeks of take out before we can do anything."

"Fuck you," Caleb answers, but he's laughing.

"Not yet."

How the fuck is he supposed to take that?

℘℃℘

SCOTT answers the door and pulls him into a hug as soon as the door closes behind him.

"Sorry we took so long. Won't happen again," Scott mumbles in his ear before he steps back.

"S'okay."

Chris hands him a beer when he gets to the living room, and he can't help raising an eyebrow.

"Trying to get me drunk again?"

"You get drunk off one beer now?"

"Chris just can't have a conversation without beer." Scott smiles, but it's tense, not the easy, loose smile Caleb's used to.

"Guys, look, we don't have to talk about it. We were drunk, and stuff happened, but it's no big deal." He's had two weeks to practice this speech. It only took three days to decide that he didn't want to risk losing either of them as friends.

"You saying you don't want it to happen again?" Chris asks, glancing over at Scott before taking a long pull from his bottle.

Caleb stares down at his bottle. He wasn't prepared for that question. He knows Chris. He knows how Chris feels about Scott, and he's not really into being the odd one out. Sure, the last time

25

was hot, but he's not used to being left alone on the couch after a hook up.

"We don't want it to be like last time," Chris says. When Caleb looks up, he's nodding to Scott.

"It wouldn't be us together and you on the side. We don't want that. We know you wouldn't put up with that shit."

"So what are we talking about?" It's not fair. They had two weeks to figure out what they wanted, and he doesn't have a clue in hell what they want from him.

Scott shrugs. "We try it... with all three of us. We both want you, and we don't want to break up, so.... "

He wants to tell them they're crazy. People don't do that. They make shows about it on cable, sure, but real people don't have relationships with more than one person at a time and act like it's okay. Except that he figured out that Chris was crazy a long time ago.

"Or we can forget it all and go back to how things were. It's up to you." Chris takes another pull from his beer and bites his lip. Caleb's never seen him nervous before.

This was really the last thing he expected. He thought maybe they might want to hook up with him again, and he was prepared to turn them down. He'd also considered that they wanted to forget it ever happened, or hell, that they'd want to forget about him all together.

"You don't have to answer now," Scott says. That's what makes up his mind. What if he waits? They're not going to take some vow of celibacy until he decides. They're going to be together even if he says no, and he'll be the third wheel even more than he was before.

"So how does this work?" he asks, and they both break into smiles.

"I don't know. It's not like we've done this before." Chris shrugs, and that helps. It's good to know they don't just try this every few years or something.

"We'll figure it out as we go along," Scott answers. This time, *we* isn't just Chris and Scott.

"Great. Can we be finished with the talking and get to the fucking now?" Chris says, and Scott laughs.

"We've talked so much in the last two weeks; I thought Chris was going to go insane." Scott says as he pulls Caleb to his feet, letting his hands rest on Caleb's hips.

"Yeah, well, I'm not the fucking girl in this relationship," Chris answers, stepping behind Caleb and pressing against his back.

"As long as you don't think I'm the girl," Caleb adds. He's not filling the girl gap or whatever if they think they have one.

"No. Scott's the girl."

"Fuck you."

"Not tonight," Chris says behind him, running his hands under Caleb's shirt and over his chest.

"Not here." Scott looks over his shoulder at Chris. They're speaking their own language again, but Caleb's too distracted by the hands on his chest and ass to give a shit. Then Scott pulls him by the waistband of his jeans and leads them down the hall. Chris pulls Caleb's shirt over his head as they walk, following it with his own.

Scott backs onto the bed and pulls Caleb with him. Their bed. Technically, it's Scott's bed, but Caleb knows Chris only sleeps at his own place when Scott's out of town. Hell, he's pretty sure Chris still sleeps in Scott's bed half the time when he's gone.

"Hey. You okay with this?" Scott asks when he zones out. If he's having second thoughts, he should really decide now. Chris runs a hand down his back, waiting.

"Yeah." Caleb nods and moves into Scott's arms as Chris climbs on the bed behind him. Scott reaches a hand behind his neck, and he hesitates. He's seen Chris get pissed off just from someone hanging on Scott a little too long, but when he turns to look at Chris, Chris just nods, reaching past him to run his fingers through Scott's hair and pull Scott toward him.

It's just a soft touch of lips at first, but when Chris starts to mouth down the side of his neck, Caleb relaxes. He lets his lips part for Scott's tongue, deepening the kiss as he pulls Scott closer.

"So fucking hot," Chris breathes, reaching around him to run his hand over Scott's face while they kiss.

Scott still has a shirt on, and that's just not fair. Caleb fumbles with the buttons, pushing it over his shoulders without breaking the kiss. Scott's mouth is hot, and Caleb can feel Scott's hard cock against his thigh. Caleb shifts, lining up his cock with Scott's and bucking against him.

"You two better not come in your jeans," Chris says, and Caleb has to pull away to laugh. He thought this might be awkward, but it's not. It's easy and relaxed just like things with Chris and Scott have always been. Chris pulls away, and when Caleb hears the pull of a zipper behind him, he can't help turning his head back to look. Chris's cock curves hard against his stomach, and Caleb moans as Chris presses back against him.

"He's yours now too," Scott whispers in his ear, something he didn't expect to hear so soon.

Caleb works on Scott's jeans while Chris reaches around and unzips his, pulling jeans and boxer briefs off and tossing them off the bed. Caleb gets Scott's jeans over his hips, and Scott kicks the rest of his clothes over the side of the bed.

Scott presses back against him, kissing down his neck as Chris turns his head to claim his lips. Chris's kiss is harder than Scott's. His tongue pushes into Caleb's mouth, and his teeth nip at Caleb's lips, claiming him the way Caleb's seen him claim Scott. Caleb moans into his mouth, unable to keep himself from grinding his cock against Scott's.

Nothing is like he thought it would be. Even when they said it wouldn't be them as a couple with him on the side, he'd assumed he'd suck Scott off while Chris fucked Scott or something. He never thought they'd put him in the middle and just attack him from both sides.

"Wanna fuck you," Chris moans into his mouth as his hard cock presses into Caleb's back.

"Fuck, yeah." Scott says when he hesitates, not sure if that's a line Scott will want him to cross.

Scott claims his mouth again, and Caleb pushes between them, skin sliding against skin.

"Yeah," he breathes as they break the kiss.

"Done this before?" Chris asks, running his hand down Caleb's side and resting on his hip.

"Yeah... been a while, but yeah." He's never done it with two people, but he's pretty sure that's not what Chris is asking.

"Okay." Chris moves away to dig in the table by the bed, and Caleb shivers a little as the cool air rushes against his back.

Then Chris is behind him again, leaning over Caleb to pull Scott into a long kiss above Caleb's head. Their eyes lock as they pull away, and he wishes again that he could read them like they read each other. Whatever it is, they agree and kiss one more time before Scott turns his attention back to Caleb and starts to kiss down his chest. Chris's arms come around his chest, pulling him close as Scott licks over his stomach.

"Scott's good—a fucking cock slut. I think he's been wanting to get your cock in his mouth since he saw it."

Caleb moans as Scott does just that, takes Caleb's cock all the way into his mouth and *swallows* it down. Caleb struggles not to

29

buck into his mouth, and Chris must notice because his hands move down to Caleb's hips, and hold him tight against his body.

"Told you." Chris's laugh is rough as Scott pulls back, swirling his tongue over the head of Caleb's cock before sucking him down again.

"Fuck," Caleb moans, grinding his ass into Chris's cock and hoping Chris gets the point because he sure as hell can't talk.

"Getting there," Chris says. His voice is strained, not in perfect control anymore. He moves his hand off Caleb's hip, and Caleb can hear the pop as he opens the bottle of lube. Caleb's expecting Chris's fingers, but instead, Scott's hand moves over and behind his balls, wet with lube. Chris finds his mouth as Scott pushes a slick finger into his body, never stopping the assault on his cock.

Chris's tongue fucks into his mouth, and it's almost too much. Caleb's not going to last long once Chris pushes inside.

"More," he moans, pushing back on Scott's finger, and Chris's hand moves from his hip as he slicks his own fingers. Caleb bites his lip as Chris slides a finger in next to Scott's, rubbing against just the right spot until Caleb pushes back with more force, groaning and fucking himself on their fingers. Scott pulls off, like he senses Caleb won't last long enough if he doesn't, and mouths at his hip until they pull both fingers out of his body. Caleb lifts his head just in time to see Scott roll the condom on and stroke lube over Chris's cock.

Scott sits up, and Caleb watches them kiss again before Scott settles on the bed in front of him.

"Ready?" Scott asks. When Caleb nods, Scott kisses him long and slow as Chris presses inside. It's been a long time, and he has to break away from Scott to take a deep breath.

"Okay?" Scott cups Caleb's cheek in his hand. Chris pauses and kisses the back of his neck, waiting until he takes another breath and the burn eases.

"Yeah," he tells Scott, and Chris inches the rest of the way in. Scott kisses him while Chris sucks on the base of his neck until he can't take it anymore and he pushes back against Chris.

"Fuck." Chris finally loses his cool and thrusts hard. Scott kisses him through it and presses against him, letting go and grinding his cock against Caleb's.

"So hot," Chris moans. His hand reaches around Caleb, running his hand over Caleb's face and then Scott's. He pushes two fingers inside their mouths, rubbing over both tongues, and then pulls his hand out. Caleb's vaguely aware of Chris moving his hand down Scott's body, but he's too distracted by the cock in his ass and Scott's cock rubbing against his to worry about it. Scott breaks the kiss with a groan and buries his head in Caleb's neck, moaning and grinding against Caleb's cock.

Caleb forces his eyes open and looks over Scott's shoulder to see Chris fucking two fingers hard and fast into Scott. It's hot, and with Scott writhing against him, Caleb loses it. His head falls on Scott's shoulder, and he grinds against him just as hard, fucking himself on Chris's cock as he does. He comes first; scraping blunt nails down Scott's back and splattering hot against his stomach.

Scott moans out his name, rubbing his cock into the sticky mess and biting Caleb's neck as he comes.

Caleb's still mostly out of it when Chris pushes into him and comes, but he's pretty sure he hears Chris growl *mine* as he does. Chris kisses his back, and Caleb thinks that he doesn't just mean Scott anymore.

Chris pulls out slowly, and it stings, but it's kind of hard to care. They should clean up, but Caleb's pretty sure he can't move. When he opens his eyes, Scott gives him a sleepy smile.

"Lazy asses," Chris complains, but there's no heat in it, and they laugh at him together as he gets up. Chris comes back with a wet washcloth, and Caleb starts when he runs the cold cloth over him, cleaning him up first and then Scott.

"Fuck. You couldn't use hot water?" Scott says as Chris cleans the come off his stomach.

"I'm the one who got out of bed, so you can be grateful and quit your bitching." Chris tosses the towel on the floor and climbs back in next to Caleb.

Scott rolls his eyes, but Chris leans over Caleb and kisses Scott before he can say anything else. When he pulls back, Scott just smiles and falls back on the bed.

"Hey." Chris smiles and kisses Caleb next, running his hand through Caleb's short hair before moving to spoon against his back.

Scott sighs and moves into Caleb's arms, kissing him and tangling their legs together before tucking his head under Caleb's chin.

ℰℛ

THE sunlight on his face confuses Caleb when he wakes up. He hates being forced awake by sun. He moans and turns into the arms around him, burying his face into a warm body.

"Mornin'," Chris drawls above him, making him remember where he is.

"Hate light," he mumbles into Chris's chest.

"That's kind of what happens in the morning." Chris laughs and kisses the top of his head.

"You need curtains. Blackout curtains." If sleeping over is going to be a regular thing; this problem has to be fixed.

"I'll try to remember to remind Scott." Chris is making fun of him, but he's also blocking the sunlight, so Caleb decides to excuse it for now. Then he realizes what's missing.

He starts to move away from Chris, but Chris holds on.

"He's making breakfast. If we don't get up, he'll bring it in here." Chris smirks, and Caleb curls against him again. He wonders how long they've been doing this. They have all these routines, and he doesn't have a clue how he's supposed to just fit in the middle of it.

"We'll get your curtains," Chris says like he knows what Caleb's thinking, and Caleb nods into his chest.

He's drifting off when Chris speaks again. "You're cute in the morning."

"I'm not cute." Did Chris miss the memo where he was not the girl?

"Uh huh. Sure… sweetheart."

"What?" Chris cannot be serious.

"You don't like it, schnookums?" Chris deserves to get hit for that. "Hey! That's domestic abuse now."

"Why did I agree to this?" Caleb groans and pushes Chris away as Scott enters with a tray of food and coffee.

"What? I left you alone with him for twenty minutes, and he's changing his mind?" Scott rolls his eyes at Chris as he hands them both coffee.

"I'm just trying to be a good boyfriend!"

"Which means you're being an asshole," Scott says. "Stop or I'm keeping him for myself."

"Whatever. I'll buy him curtains, and he'll pick me," Chris says, but he accepts Scott's kiss as Scott hands him a plate of waffles.

"I'll stick with the original plan if Chris will shut up," Caleb says, mostly because the waffles smell good.

"Good luck with that."

CHAPTER 5

CALEB thought Scott and Chris stopped censoring themselves after he found out. Hell, they'd kissed in front of him and hugged, so really, he figured the only things they were censoring involved nudity.

Now he has to wonder what else he didn't know. Either they've been holding back all the time, or they've decided that adding him to the mix justifies a whole new honeymoon period.

It starts subtly enough. Scott curls up with him on the couch to watch TV, and that's cool. He's never been big on the cuddling part of relationships, but Scott is, and it's not like he minds. Chris bitches about the documentary he's watching even though Scott takes Caleb's side like he always does, and that's nothing new. What *is* new is that Chris decides to solve his problem by climbing into Caleb's lap to make out. Scott pushes him off, and they wrestle until they're all a tangle of limbs. Chris gives up trying to make them change the channel and passes out with his head in Caleb's lap while they watch the rest of the show.

Chris likes to kiss him at the most random times. Caleb will be on his laptop, answering his e-mail, and Chris will lean down and kiss him as he walks by. Sometimes it's not even just a kiss. He'll be standing on the porch talking to his sister on the phone, and one or *both* of them will just step behind him and hold him for a second, kiss the side of his neck, and move on.

For a while, he kind of feels like he's some kind of novelty for them, like a new toy they want to play with all the time, and he pulls away once when Scott goes to kiss him. Scott gets this hurt look in his eyes as he tries to play it off, and when Caleb looks at Chris, he expects him to be mad, but he just looks confused. So Caleb feels like an ass, coughs and apologizes, saying he just didn't want to cough on him or something. Scott laughs, and everything goes back to normal.

After that, he pays more attention to how they are together, and it's not as different as he thought. Maybe they've been pushing it with him so that he doesn't feel left out, but they're still all over each other too. Chris always messes with Scott while he cooks, trying to distract him with kisses down his neck, so he can steal bits of food before he's supposed to and always ends up getting some of the sauce on Scott's face so that he can lick it off. Scott swats him, laughing and begging Caleb to take him away. He does until Scott is making cookies and forbids them to sample the cookie dough.

Caleb still sleeps at his place by himself sometimes. He knows they aren't happy about it even before he overhears Scott telling Chris that he needs to chill out. This is all still new for Caleb. He watches as Scott pulls Chris into a kiss and tells him to relax, that Caleb will come around if Chris stops pushing. And he hates that he's making this hard for them, but Scott's right. This *is* new for him. He hasn't been in this relationship for years like they have, and he can't jump straight into practically living at Scott's apartment like Chris does.

Scott gets it, even if he doesn't really like it. He kisses Caleb goodbye at the end of the night and pulls Chris away before he starts to complain about it. Sometimes, they go to Caleb's, and Chris always bitches that Caleb's bed is too soft and too far off the ground. He says he spends the whole night trying not to roll off the side, but when Caleb offers to let him sleep in the middle, he shakes his head. Caleb's not sure if it's because they already had sides of the bed claimed, but he kind of likes sleeping between them anyway.

❧❧

CHRIS spends the first three weeks trying to call him stupid pet names. Caleb doesn't even know how he comes up with most of them or how Chris keeps a straight face while calling him *cuddle bear* for an entire day. Chris drops the name after Caleb threatens to withhold sex, which is good because he still hasn't figured out if he would have to withhold sex from Scott too.

Of course, that just makes him wonder again if they still have sex when he's not there, and he can't think about that because he decided earlier that he's going home to his own apartment today. He has a shoot tomorrow, and they'll keep him up late if he stays.

"They're going to love you, and they're going to want to hire you again," Scott says before he kisses Caleb goodnight and leaves him alone with Chris. He gives Chris a look as he leaves, but Caleb's starting to get their looks now. This one tells Chris to let him leave without bitching about it.

"He's always right. I don't know why I even bother meeting with people when he has a bad feeling."

"You realize this makes you go into it thinking people won't like your pictures, and that might have something to do with it, right?" Caleb asks, and Chris rolls his eyes.

"You can't go psych major on me. You didn't even *start* college. I took Intro to psych freshman year."

"It's not my fault I got an internship out of high school."

"Well we can't all be so gifted that *TeenChic* hires us out of high school. Some of us have to go to college, shoot a lot of weddings, and play in run down bars."

36

Caleb laughs and tilts his head up for a kiss. Chris deepens the kiss, and Caleb knows it's the only way Chris can ask him to stay without really asking, but he pulls away and says goodnight anyway.

He puts his guitar in the passenger seat. When he walks back around and gets in the truck, the cab light stays on, letting him know he didn't close the other door all the way. He leans over to pop it open and slam it closed all the way, and he's not even sure how the fuck it happens. He has no idea why he doesn't realize bracing himself with his hand on the door frame wasn't a good idea. All he knows is that it hurts like fuck when he slams the door on all four fingers of his left hand.

"Fuck!" He has no idea how loud he yells it the first time, but he's still repeating it when Chris opens the driver's side door.

"What the fuck are you cussing about?" Chris asks, pulling him back out of the trunk.

"Slammed my hand in the door," he manages. He'd feel like an idiot if he could feel anything besides his hand.

Chris reaches past him to get his guitar because he knows Caleb won't just leave his guitar in the truck; then he leads him back inside.

His fingers are scraped and bleeding just a little. His whole hand is throbbing, and he's pretty sure his fingers weren't that big a minute ago.

Chris pulls him into the kitchen and uses a wet rag to clean off the blood. There isn't much, and it doesn't soak through the towel when Chris leaves him to make an ice pack. Chris holds the ice pack on his hand even when he tries to jerk away. It's a fucking reflex. Ice never feels good until it makes everything go numb.

They sit at the breakfast bar in silence for a few minutes, Chris's thumb rubbing light circles on his wrist.

"Dude. They're broken. We should just go to the hospital." This is lame. He's going to have to reschedule because he can't hold a camera. "I'm going to have to learn how to play chords with my thumb. Or I can be one of those people who only plays one chord."

He expects Chris to call him a drama queen and laugh, but Chris just smiles a little and sets the ice pack aside. Caleb almost pulls away, but Chris is gentle as he feels over each finger. The bleeding has stopped, and his fingers don't look so swollen anymore. Chris leans over and kisses his lips. "I really think you're okay, darlin'."

He should complain and tell Chris he means it about withholding sex if he doesn't stop with the stupid pet names, but Chris is just watching him with this worried look like he doesn't even know he said it. Caleb figures *darlin'* is better than *cuddle bear*, so he sighs and leans his head against Chris's chest instead.

"Come to bed?" Chris asks, and kisses the top of his head, like Caleb was really going to drive home now.

He nods and lets Chris lead him to the bedroom and strip off his clothes. Scott stirs a little when he climbs under the covers, but he doesn't wake up. When Caleb looks back, he sees Chris setting the alarm for his shoot. Chris spoons behind him and kisses the back of his neck, and he wonders why he was so insistent about going home in the first place.

ℰℭ

CALEB wakes up to the feeling of a hand rubbing wide circles into his back. Even though he really doesn't want to get up, it's better than jolting up to an alarm. Scott always wakes up with the sun, and that hasn't changed since they got thicker curtains for the window, so Scott's taken to watching the clock and waking him up before the alarm whenever he stays over. He should remember this next time he decides to be independent and sleep at his own place.

Scott's smiling when Caleb finally caves and opens his eyes.

"Hey."

"Hey," Caleb whispers back. Chris isn't awake yet, and he hates being woken early for no reason.

"Thought you were going home?"

"Change of plans," he answers, and Scott's eyebrows rise in question. "I kind of hurt my hand as I was going. Didn't feel like driving."

"Hurt your hand?" Scott's hand reaches down and finds his, pulling it over the blanket. It's bruised, but it doesn't look half as bad as it did the night before. "Shit. Baby, how'd you do this?"

Scott's not like Chris with pet names. Caleb's pretty sure he actively tries not to use them because Caleb bitches at Chris so much, but sometimes he slips, and Caleb can't bring himself to be annoyed when Scott's not doing it just to piss him off like Chris does.

"Closed my hand in the door of my truck. It's all right. No big deal." He hopes Chris won't be an asshole and tell the real story about how he whined and thought his hand was broken.

"Sorry about your hand." Scott smiles and pulls Caleb's hand to his lips. "But I'm glad you stayed."

Caleb doesn't really know what he's supposed to say to that. He never really does when Scott comes out with shit like that, but maybe Scott knows because he pulls back before it can get too awkward.

"So, you want breakfast?"

ℂ℃

AFTER the shoot, Caleb goes home to change and shower. He's determined to stay home and do something, anything that has nothing to do with Scott or Chris, because he really didn't mean to spend the night. He's spent seven days in his own bed in the three weeks since he agreed to this relationship, and three of those days he had Chris and Scott in the bed with him. He needs to get some damn distance before he gets tied into this thing only to find out that they just want to be with each other after all.

Because Chris and Scott? They're a unit. And sure, they say he's equal in this relationship, but it's still like he's dating them as a couple. Part of that might be his fault, because it's not like they want him to sleep at his own apartment, or go out and get wasted with Jason and not answer their calls until the next day, though he probably shouldn't do that again unless he really wants out. It wasn't worth the look on Scott's face or the way Chris glared daggers at him until Scott calmed Chris down.

But that's the thing. They're a team. Even with him, they're a team. They decided they wanted to let him into their relationship, but it's still just that—*their* relationship.

When the phone rings, he's not really surprised. Scott told him to let them know how it went before he left, and they've got to know the shoot is long over.

"Hey."

"Next time Scott gives me his stupid lecture about giving you space, I'm going to remind him that *I* just spent the last hour telling him to just wait until you called."

"So you called?"

"No. This is all him. I just had to tell you that before I gave him the phone."

"Asshole," he hears Scott mumble as he takes the phone. "Hey. I just wanted to ask how the shoot went."

"Good. I think they liked me, but you never know."

"I think they loved you. You'll get something big out of this," Scott says, and then he yells, "Christopher King, step away from the cheese or I will make myself dinner and let you have just cheese."

"What? Are we on war rations? If Caleb's not coming—in any way—I should get to eat his food." Chris yells back loud enough for Caleb to hear.

"Because I couldn't possibly save it for later?" Caleb can imagine Scott rolling his eyes before he speaks into the phone again. "Have you eaten at all since you skipped breakfast?"

When Caleb doesn't answer, Scott sighs. It's not like he meant to not eat all day. He just can't eat when he gets up too early, and then he got really busy playing video games.

"Caleb, come eat dinner? I'll make sure he lets you go home if you want to. I know you don't have anything to eat at your place."

Caleb can't help laughing. "Yes, *Mom*."

ᑏᑐ

CALEB feels like he should be doing something. Scott cooked, which means Chris has to do the dishes. He knows this. He's had their routines down for a while now, but at some point, he should be helping with something.

At first, Scott said he was a guest, but Chris was long past being a guest and damn well had to work for his dinner. But it's been months since he started eating most of his meals at Scott's and almost a month since he started sleeping here, and Scott still pulls him out of the kitchen while Chris cleans up.

"Heading home?" Scott asks.

Caleb means to say yes, he's going home to sleep in his own bed, but he thinks maybe the reason they still treat him like a guest is because he still acts like one.

"I was kind of thinking I might stick around for the Rangers game." He's not a huge fan of baseball, but since he moved to LA, watching Texas teams makes him feel less homesick. It helps that Chris is from Texas, too, and he still cheers for the Rangers even though he deserted to Oklahoma after middle school.

Scott groans, but he pulls Caleb to the couch. "Not that Chris wasn't going to make me watch it if you left, but you're supposed to take my side when it comes to the TV."

"It's only going to get worse in football season." Caleb laughs as Scott lies down on the couch and pulls Caleb down with him, spooning against his back and snaking an arm under his shirt. It's a tight fit, and he's pretty sure Scott can't see the TV, but Scott probably doesn't care.

"At least shit happens in football," Scott says, but Caleb can imagine his smile just before Scott presses kisses into his back. It's been a while since they did this. He didn't mean to, but he's been leaving pretty much every day they don't have sex. If he's honest, he's been coming over for nothing but sex or food for the last week too. Scott never says anything, but Caleb knows it bothers Scott when he doesn't spend time just hanging out. He saw it in the way Scott watched him when he woke up this morning, like he didn't expect Caleb to be there if he wasn't too worn out from sex to go home.

"Shit happens in baseball."

"Once an hour?" Scott asks. He rubs slow circles over Caleb's chest, and Caleb snuggles closer in Scott's arms without thinking.

"Good thing I can crash here if it runs late."

"Yeah." He feels Scott kiss the back of his neck just as Chris walks in.

"Where the hell am I supposed to sit with y'all taking up the whole fucking couch?" he asks, but he's smiling as he reaches down to run his hand over Scott's hair. Scott sits up a little, pulling Caleb with him just enough to make room for Chris to sit down before letting his head fall on Chris's lap.

Caleb's watched games with them before. Scott hates baseball, and he always falls asleep with his head on Chris's lap in the first inning. Before, Caleb always watched them from the chair across the room, but now he lets his head fall on Chris's lap just in front of Scott's.

"One of you is blowing me later if I'm going to sit like this the whole game," Chris says.

"If you don't get pissed off at the game and wake me up with your yelling like you did last time," Scott answers as he pulls Caleb close again and relaxes.

Chris and Caleb watch the game in silence until Scott is snoring between them.

"He sleeps better when you're here," Chris says. Caleb's not sure what he's supposed to say to that, so he just nods and tries to concentrate on the game.

CHAPTER 6

CALEB has an idea of what everyone else thinks about his thing with Chris and Scott—not that any of their friends have mentioned anything to him. He knows Chris told everyone who mattered at some point. And if they didn't know about Chris and Scott in the first place, what's going on with Caleb is none of their business. But he also knows that Chris hasn't left him alone with Jason since the whole thing started.

Chris and Scott are playing together tonight, though, so he'll be on his own while they're on stage.

"See you after the show?" Chris asks as he moves away from the group. His hand rests on the small of Caleb's back, and Caleb rolls his eyes.

"Think I'm gonna leave you here?'

"Naw, you'd never leave Scott. You'd probably starve to death." Chris smirks and walks off to where Scott has already started to set up.

Everything is normal for the first half of the show. Bullshitting with the guys has never really been work for him. He gets up to get another beer, and when Jason follows him, he doesn't think anything about it.

"Caleb? Can I say something that might piss you off?" Jason asks, leaning close so he can be heard over the music. That alone is enough to tell Caleb how this is going to go. He could say no, but all that's going to do is keep their friends talking behind his back.

"Say what you want. Can't promise I won't get pissed off anyway." He takes his beer from the bartender and hands the other to Jason. He's not drunk enough for this, but Jason probably is, because he leans his shoulder on Caleb as he talks.

"I've known Chris and Scott a while. I remember when they broke up the last time and how awful it was until they got back together," he starts. Caleb just nods because this is all stuff he knows. He came in late. He knows that. "The thing is... they have this habit of trying out new things. Toys, drugs, and weird sexual positions I wish they wouldn't tell me about when they get high. And they have fun, but they always get bored of whatever new thing and go back to the basics until they get bored with that again."

"You think I'm just some new thing they're trying out?" It's not like he hasn't thought of this himself.

"I don't know, but maybe." Jason sighs and leans even closer so that Caleb can hear him over the music. "I really hope it's not like that, but I just want you to be careful. You're the one that could really get hurt in this thing, you know?"

"I know. I'm being careful. You don't have to get all mother hen on me," he says, grinning and shoving Jason a little. Jason tries to push him back, but his feet aren't steady, and he stumbles, staying upright only because Caleb catches him around the waist and holds him up.

"All right, all right. I'm just saying call me if it goes to hell. I know you. You'll go hide in your apartment and starve to death."

"I'm not that pathetic. I'd order food." Really. He hasn't found the best hot wings yet. Except that he doesn't really like hot wings.

"That you'd never eat."

45

"Fuck you," Caleb answers, but he has to laugh. When Jason laughs too, the stress of the conversation falls, and they stand in silence, listening to the last three songs.

The set is finished, but he doesn't move to the stage. It always takes them a few minutes to break everything down, and it's been a while since he's really gotten to talk to Jason without Chris or Scott hanging over his shoulder.

"So things are really good? With them? Because you have to know the whole thing sounds really weird."

"Yeah. I know, but it's good. It's not weird. I know it sounds like it should be, but it just kind of works with all three of us."

"He seriously lets you touch Scott? And you're not worried he'll kill you in your sleep after?"

"He lets me touch *his guitar*." Caleb laughs at Jason's expression, and he feels Chris come up before he sees him. Chris wraps an arm around Caleb, his palm pressing flat against Caleb's chest as he's pulled away from Jason.

Caleb relaxes against his chest. He's just about to turn around and tell Chris it was a great show when Jason says, "Hey, man, we were just talking."

"Looked like a bit more than talking to me," Chris says. Caleb tries to turn around so he can tell Chris he's being an idiot. It's *Jason*. Their *friend*. Not some random chick in a bar. But Chris is holding him too tightly for him to turn around without actually shoving Chris away. And that would start a whole new fight. He relaxes when he sees Scott out of the corner of his eye.

"Maybe you should try asking Caleb before you go fucking crazy," Scott says, stepping between them and Jason. Scott pulls Chris's hand away, and Chris only resists a little before he lets Caleb go to Scott.

"S'okay," Scott says into his ear, wrapping an arm around Caleb's waist as Caleb turns to face Chris.

"We were just talking. You should fucking know that. We're friends. I'm allowed to have friends. Not to mention that Jason is your friend too."

Chris glances between him and Jason before answering. "He should fucking know better."

It's kind of true, and that's the only reason Caleb sighs and lets Chris pull him back against his side. They all know not to hang too much on Scott, so they should know not to hang all over him either. Hell, Caleb spent the first few days of their relationship shocked that Chris was letting him anywhere near Scott, but that doesn't mean he's okay with Chris bitching at Jason for no reason, either.

"We were still just talking. You should trust me," Caleb says. Chris nods but doesn't give him a real answer.

"Good. Let's just go home, okay?" Scott says, and Caleb's pretty sure he's not the only one mouthing *sorry* to Jason. Jason just shrugs and nods. He can always call Jason and apologize for his crazy, jealous boyfriend later, but he's pretty sure he sees a smirk on Jason's face as he walks away, so he figures they'll all forget about it by tomorrow. And if Chris holds him tighter than normal as they walk outside, he's not really complaining.

They're all quiet on the ride home, but Chris never really lets him go. His hand runs over Caleb's leg and up his arm, and then it rests on the back of Caleb's neck until they get to Scott's house. He expects Chris to let go when they get out of the car, but Chris nods to Scott to get both of their guitars while he leads Caleb inside with a hand on his back. Scott goes in first and sets down their guitars, and there's a smirk on his face when he reaches out to pull Caleb in by the waistband of his jeans.

Chris crowds in behind Caleb, pressing up against his back and kissing down his neck as Scott leads them to the bedroom. Scott's smirking the entire time, like he knows something Caleb doesn't. Caleb wonders if he should be worried, but Scott's never hurt him yet.

Scott lies down on the bed and pulls Caleb down with him as he pops open the button to Caleb's jeans. Chris climbs on the bed after them, stripping off his own clothes, but he backs off for the first time since he dragged Caleb out of the club and props himself up on his elbow to watch them. Scott's hands run through Caleb's hair, and he pulls Caleb's lips to his, kissing him hard before nipping down Caleb's jaw to his ear and sucking on the lobe.

"*This* is why I put up with his crazy possessive bullshit." Scott's still smirking as he pushes Caleb over onto his back. Caleb's planning to reach for Chris, but Chris is on top of him before he can, kissing him hard and fucking Caleb's mouth with his tongue. His hands push up Caleb's shirt enough for Scott to pull it off, fingers digging into Caleb's skin as he mouths down Caleb's neck.

He's going to push Chris away. He's damn well seen Scott try to cover up hickeys with his hair, and Caleb knows he doesn't have any hair to cover up the spot behind his ear Chris moves on to. Everyone is going to be able to see it, but he's pretty sure that's the point. He pulls his hands up to shove at Chris's chest, but Chris chooses that moment to reach into his jeans and grip his cock, making Caleb groan and grip his arms instead.

"Scott can touch you. I can touch you," Chris says as he lifts his hips just enough for Scott to pull off Caleb's jeans and boxer-briefs. Caleb tries to form a response, to remind Chris that he's insane and Jason wasn't even doing anything, but Chris pulls on his cock again as he continues. "No one else gets to fucking touch you."

Chris kisses him hard, and he gives up. He'll get Chris back later; for now, he cares more about Chris's cock pushing against his. Scott comes back, naked against him, to chew on the side of his neck as Chris pulls away from the kiss so he can mark the other side. Caleb's not really sure when Scott lost his clothes, but he's not complaining as Scott reaches behind his balls with sticky-wet fingers and presses into him.

"Good?" Scott asks, feeling with his fingers until Caleb whines and shivers.

"Fuck. Yeah." It's all Caleb can do to reach out and tangle his fingers in Scott's hair, pulling Scott's mouth to his.

He's pushing his tongue into Scott's mouth when Chris turns and pushes his tongue in the middle. They don't kiss like this much. After a while, it's always too many noses fighting for air, but Caleb still loves it when Chris goes for it, like seeing the two of them kissing gets him so hot that he can't help but push in.

Scott pulls away first, which is good because Caleb was having a little trouble breathing, and he can't really move with Chris pressing him into the bed and Scott at his side. Scott's fingers slide out of his ass, and Caleb can't help whimpering into Chris's mouth at the loss. Chris, the bastard, chuckles and sits up as Scott rolls the condom over his cock.

"Hold on, darlin'. Gonna fuck you good," Chris growls in his ear as Scott slicks him up and grips Caleb's cock with his still slick hand. Caleb bucks into Scott's hand as Chris pulls up his legs and pushes inside. It's quick, but Caleb's had him enough now to relax and go with it. Chris stills for a second, and none of them say anything, but he knows they're watching him, making sure he's fine before Chris starts to thrust, pushing in again and again in time with Scott's hand.

Chris is starting to lose it, thrusting into him as he bites down on Caleb's shoulder. Caleb's pretty far gone when he decides Scott's not gone enough. He reaches out, finds Scott's cock with his hand, and pulls, rough and quick like he knows Scott likes it. Scott moves closer, and Caleb turns his head, licking up Scott's neck and sucking hard. It's not fair if he ends up the only one all marked up.

Scott groans, burying his face in Caleb's neck as he thrusts into Caleb's fist and spills over Caleb's hand. His grip on Caleb's cock tightens, and that's what ends it. Caleb splashes come over Scott's hand and his own.

"So fucking hot," Chris bites out. When he pushes in hard and stills, Caleb forces his eyes open to watch Chris's face as Chris comes inside him.

Chris falls on his chest, breathing hot on his neck, and he's pretty sure Chris mumbles *mine* into his skin a few times. Possessive bastard.

"Man, you can't fall asleep like this." Caleb's kind of tempted to let him, but he knows that as good as it feels to have Chris covering him now, it'll feel like hell in the morning.

Chris grunts and rolls off him, slipping out all the way and falling on his side. He pulls off the condom and tosses it in the trash by the bed. "Scott? You gotta get up."

"You topped. That makes it your job," Scott says, but he gives in when Caleb turns to him and pouts. There's no way he's waking up covered in dried come, and Chris isn't moving. Caleb closes his eyes as Scott wipes them off and turns on his side so Chris can spoon behind him. Chris is breathing evenly against his back when Scott climbs in bed and kisses Caleb goodnight. Caleb smiles as Scott pulls back and settles in next to him.

"You make him jealous on purpose sometimes, don't you?" Caleb asks. Scott smiles but doesn't answer.

CHAPTER 7

CHRIS is still snoring when Caleb wakes up the next morning, but Scott is already gone, probably making the first pot of coffee. Caleb slips out from under Chris's arm, and Chris whines in his sleep, reaching for him. Caleb worries he might wake up, but when Caleb finds a pillow to put under his arm, Chris relaxes back into sleep. Later, Caleb's going to point out what a sap he really is.

He can hear Scott singing in the kitchen as he slips out the door to sit on the stairs outside. The morning air is cool, and he probably should have found more than last night's smoky jeans and a thin white T-shirt.

Last night, he was too distracted to think about what Jason said, and he wants to think what happened proves that Chris and Scott aren't just playing around. He wants to think Chris wouldn't get so jealous if he was just the latest thing to put a spark in their sex life, but he doesn't *know* that.

His phone vibrates in his pocket, and he's kind of amazed it didn't fall out at some point when they were pulling off his jeans. It's Dan. It has to be good if he's calling this early in the morning. Dan knows better than to wake him up with bad news.

"Hey."

"You're awake?"

"Couldn't sleep."

"Please tell me whatever's keeping you from sleeping isn't going to make you act like an asshole and piss everyone off again." Dan acts like this happens often instead of the one or two times it has. He's more professional than that.

"No, I'm fine. What's up?"

"I showed a friend of mine your pictures. Wilkes wants you in New York to shoot the new spring lines for *Chic*." *Chic* isn't exactly new to him, but it's a good deal considering that he doesn't want to be nailed down. It's better than going to fashion week alone and hoping he might get into the right shows to get some good shots that he can sell later.

"Great. Thanks, man." He means it. Dan puts up with his shit and still talks him up to the right people. "When do I need to be there?"

"They want you in New York in three days. They're putting you up until after fashion week."

"Three days? Fashion week is next month." He was planning to go anyway and see what he could get, but he wasn't planning to leave for weeks.

"They're running a story on that designer from the reality show, and they want the same photographer on the whole thing. Plus, I think Wilkes misses you. She's been trying to get you back since you were both stuck at *TeenChic*."

"Yeah," Caleb wonders if Wilkes was just waiting for an excuse to call him again anyway. "Thanks."

He manages a goodbye to Dan, and he's pretty sure Dan thinks he's thrilled. And he is, but three days? He thought he'd have more time. Hell, he didn't think anything would even come from shooting a few pictures of the model Dan just signed. Even if he isn't a phase, how can he expect Chris and Scott to just sit around waiting for the times he can get off and come home?

When did he start thinking of Chris and Scott as home? If Jason's worries are right, he's really screwed. Either way, he's been outside for a while. One of them will notice he's gone soon.

ℰℑℭℜ

SCOTT'S putting eggs and bacon on plates when Caleb comes inside. Scott's shirtless and barefoot with his loose pajama pants sitting low on his hips.

"Hey. You're up already?"

"Dan called."

"Yeah?" Scott eyes him as he sets a mug of coffee in front of him on the counter. "He didn't like the pictures?"

"No, he did. One of his friends liked them too." Caleb takes a sip of his coffee.

"Oh, man, that's great." Scott pauses when he doesn't answer, "It's great, right?"

"Yeah. It's awesome. They want me to shoot fashion week for *Chic*."

"So? Why do you look like you're dreading it?"

Caleb shrugs. It's not like they've ever really promised him anything.

"Is it about whatever Jason said to you last night?" Scott asks, and Caleb looks up. He kind of assumed they didn't see anything except how much Jason was hanging on him. "I was watching you guys too. I just see different things than Chris. I know he's been worried about you."

Caleb shrugs again and looks down at the counter. It's not fair to send them after Jason just because he was worried.

"I'm not going to get mad at Jason. I get why he'd worry. He'd be a shitty friend to you if he didn't."

"You think Chris will agree with that?" Chris was pissed off at Jason just for having an arm around his shoulders.

"Jason knows Chris. He knew what he was doing. But if you're worried, I won't tell Chris if we can just work it out now," Scott says.

"Does that mean you'll tell Chris if I don't tell you what he said?" Apparently, Scott plays dirty. He probably should have seen that coming, considering how long Scott's put up with Chris.

"Baby, what else am I supposed to do? He comes out here and finds out you're all set for fashion week, and you look like that? He's going to know something is up anyway." Scott reaches across the bar and traces over Caleb's wrist with his fingers.

"Jason said he's worried because he's seen you guys go through phases with stuff before."

"And he thinks you're just a phase to us?"

"He didn't say what he thinks. Just that he was worried about it."

"Do *you* think that?"

Caleb's not really sure he has an answer for that. "How would you even know? It's not like any of us have done this before, and I'm going to be gone a lot for this job."

"And you think what? That we'll get over you because you're not here all the time?" When Caleb doesn't answer, Scott comes around the counter and turns the barstool Caleb is sitting on so he can stand between Caleb's legs. "Caleb, I can't promise you that this is going to be perfect. But Chris and I have done distance before when he's gone on tour without me, and you're a *person*, not a new toy Chris ordered online. We wanted to be with *you*, not just any random guy off the street we could add in to spice up our sex life. If it doesn't work out, it's not because it's a phase, and I can promise you that we're going to try like hell to make this work."

"Yeah?" Caleb feels himself smiling.

"Yeah." Scott moves closer and presses their lips together. Caleb opens to him, letting Scott control the kiss. It's long and slow, and it says everything he really needs to hear.

"This? This right here is why Caleb is supposed to stay in bed with me," Chris says, and they break apart, laughing as he bitches. "My food is probably cold now, and you can't just warm up cold eggs. They'll taste funny."

"I'll make new eggs." Scott rolls his eyes at Chris, who's smiling anyway, and leans down to kiss Caleb again until Chris pulls him away.

"You cook. I'll keep Caleb company. Looks like his eggs are cold too." Chris smirks and trades places with Scott, running his hands over Caleb's thighs as he steps between them. "So why are you up early, anyway? The bed was cold when I woke up."

"Dan called. He got me a job for fashion week," Caleb tells him.

"Yeah? What magazine?" Chris grins wide, and this time Caleb smiles just as much.

"*Chic.*"

"Shit. They must've loved you." Chris doesn't know there's already a history. He just thinks it's like any of the other magazines that have grabbed him for special shoots.

Caleb shrugs. It's not like he can say *yeah, because I'm amazing*, even if he knows Chris would say it. Chris rolls his eyes, but at least he doesn't say any of his shit about how Caleb should know what an awesome photographer he is. He just leans in and kisses Caleb, licking inside his mouth until Caleb can't help moaning.

"Gonna let it get cold again?" They break apart at the clatter of plates on the counter.

"Naw. We need fuel." Chris says, and he takes the stool next to Caleb to eat. "So New York, right?"

"Yeah." Caleb exchanges a look with Scott, and Scott nods.

"You gotta leave soon?"

"Three days."

"*Three days*?" Chris puts his fork down—always a bad sign. "For how long?"

"They're putting me in a hotel until after fashion week, but I don't really know my schedule yet. I'm covering an article, plus the preparations, and then all the shows." Losing his appetite for Scott's cooking is just wrong.

"You'll probably still get weekends off?" Chris says, and Caleb smiles. Scott was right. Scott's always right.

"Yeah, so I can probably fly back a couple times."

Chris nods and doesn't say anything, but he's smiling when he picks up his fork again.

They sit in silence as they finish breakfast, and it's not until Chris leaves to take the dishes to the sink that Caleb notices the three dark hickeys on Scott's neck.

"You know, you made one of them yourself," Scott points out when he catches Caleb staring.

"At least you can cover them up," Caleb says. Scott's got his hair pulled back now, but Caleb knows he'll take it down before they go anywhere. Caleb's pretty much screwed.

"Why do you think I keep my hair long?" Scott grins as he reaches out and runs his thumb over the hickey he can take credit for on the side of Caleb's neck.

"I'd look like I'm eighteen with long hair." Caleb sighs as Scott pushes up his T-shirt and presses kisses to the hickeys Chris sucked into his chest. At least maybe Chris won't worry if he's going to go to New York with proof that he's taken all over his neck. He should kill Chris for making him go to work looking like a whore. And maybe Scott, too, because there's another mark right by the waist of his jeans Scott made when he was stripping them off.

"I'm not sure if I look like I got in a fight or had really hot sex."

"Really hot sex. Definitely."

"You say that because you were there."

"What'd you think when I looked like this before?" Scott smiles and pushes off Caleb's shirt.

"That Chris had jealousy issues, but now I know you make him like that on purpose because you're a freak."

"You gonna tell him that?"

"You're not telling him what Jason said, so we'll call it even." Caleb glances back at the kitchen to make sure Chris can't hear them.

"Deal." Scott laughs and leans in to kiss him. Caleb's pressing closer when Chris's arms wrap around his waist, and he feels Chris's lips on his neck. He slips from between them before he loses his senses again.

"Hey!" Chris frowns as he steps away.

"Man, I gotta leave in three days. I'm already marked up enough." Not that he doesn't enjoy it, but he has to have some rules.

"That's why they have makeup." Chris smirks, trying to pull him back. When he glares back, Chris tries pouting; it always looks completely fake when he's *trying*.

"I'm the photographer. Not the model." Caleb rolls his eyes and glances over Chris's body. That's when he realizes that Chris doesn't have a mark on him. He figured he or Scott made something at some point last night, but no, there's nothing.

57

"But they look so hot on you. You *should* be the model," Chris tries, and that's it.

"Maybe I think they'd look hot on you, but I wouldn't know because you don't have a fucking mark on you."

Chris freezes as Caleb glances at Scott and sees him taking his own survey of Chris's body.

"I think maybe Caleb's on to something." Scott's looking at Caleb when he says it, and Caleb takes that as cue to move behind Chris as Scott steps forward, trapping Chris between them.

"Guys? This isn't *my* fault. It's not like I could do it myself," Chris says as Caleb pushes him toward the bedroom. Maybe he has a point, but that doesn't mean he's off the hook.

"Yeah, so we really should fix this," Caleb says as he pushes off Chris's boxers, letting his palms run over Chris's ass.

"Exactly." Scott pushes off his own pants and pulls Chris on the bed with him as Caleb strips off his jeans. It's probably better that he lets Scott take the lead anyway. He's ganged up on Scott with Chris before, and he was shocked as hell the first time they let him fuck Scott. Chris is a whole new game.

But Scott seems confident as he kisses down Chris's neck and settles on a place to suck, so Caleb climbs on the bed and takes the other side, reaching down to pull on his cock when Chris starts to protest. Chris moans and pushes into his fist as Caleb kisses down his chest, stopping to swirl his tongue around Chris's nipple.

"Fuck," Chris moans as he sucks hard on the nub. So Chris likes to have his nipples played with. He never would have guessed that, and Chris sure as hell wouldn't tell him. Scott moves behind Chris's ear, and Caleb smiles as he shifts his mouth to suck another mark into Chris's chest before nipping further down.

Caleb stops to suck at Chris's hip and has to press him down into the mattress when his cock bumps into Caleb's cheek. Caleb moves back and chuckles when Chris curses.

"Fucker," Chris bitches, but Scott cuts him off when he licks into Chris's mouth, and his hand moves down Chris's chest to help Caleb hold him down as Caleb teases with licks and bites up his thigh.

"Fuck! I don't fuckin' tease you this much." Chris's hand tangles in Caleb's hair, not pulling, but Caleb still gets the point, and Chris *is* right, so Caleb moves back to swirl his tongue over the head of Chris's cock. Chris moans and lets out a string of curse words when Caleb takes him into his mouth.

He's sucked Scott off more than Chris. Usually, Chris is too busy trying to get in his ass or Scott's to get his dick sucked, but that must not be a reflection of how much he likes it. It takes both Caleb's hands and Scott's to hold Chris down. Caleb can't help wanting to see what other noises he can get out of Chris's mouth as he bobs his head and reaches down to take Chris's balls in his hand, getting a grunt he's never heard before. He doesn't notice Chris is taking short, quick breaths until Scott reaches down to pull him up.

"Not yet," Scott says as he crawls back up Chris body. Chris can't blame him for this one. Obviously, Scott is the evil one.

"Ass," Chris mumbles, but his hand runs over Caleb's back as Scott pulls him across Chris's body for a wet kiss. Scott cocks his head toward the nightstand, and Caleb pauses even though Scott is already pushing at Chris to roll over. Chris refuses to move at first, and Scott kisses him hard before trying again. Their eyes meet, and Scott brushes his thumb over Chris's cheek before kissing him. When Scott tries again, Chris rolls over to face Caleb, and Scott looks at Caleb and nods.

He's not even the one fucking Chris, and he still fumbles finding a condom and the lube in the drawer. He was starting to think Chris never did this, and maybe Chris hasn't offered it to him yet, but if he's letting Scott, maybe Caleb has a shot.

When he turns back, Chris isn't looking at him, and for the first time since he watched them fuck on the couch, he feels like maybe he should leave.

"Caleb," Scott says, getting his attention and holding out his hand until Caleb hands him the lube and the condom. Scott mouths *kiss him*, and Caleb looks back up at Chris with his head down. Scott nods again, and it hits him that it's not all that different than how Scott just looked at Chris, so he nods back and lies down facing Chris.

"Hey," he whispers, pulling Chris to look at him with a hand on his cheek. Chris bites his lip, and fuck, he can't believe the look in Chris's eyes. It's ridiculous. Chris has fucked him how many times, and he thinks Caleb's going to, what? Call him weak or girly or something?

"You're an idiot," he says, and he kisses Chris long and hard until Chris kisses back. When he pulls away, Chris still doesn't look sure, but he smiles and meets Caleb's eyes until Scott starts sucking on his shoulder and his eyes slip closed. Caleb relaxes and kisses down Chris's neck, forming a new bruise at the base as Chris moans in his ear.

Caleb strokes his hand down Chris's side and kneads at the tense muscles at the small of Chris's back. Chris shifts, and his cock rubs against Caleb's thigh. That's better. When he kisses Chris again, Chris kisses back hard, rubbing his cock hard against Caleb's leg.

Scott takes his hand from Chris's back, and Caleb doesn't know what to expect, but it's not for Scott to rub lube over his fingers and direct them down. Shit. He trusts Scott to know Chris, though. He has since this whole thing started, so he runs his thumb down the side of Chris's ass so Chris will know it's him and moves back to kiss Chris again as he trails slick fingers down Chris's ass.

He pulls back and locks eyes with Chris as he rubs over his hole. He never thought he'd be watching for something like this, but if Chris isn't okay with it, he's got to know. But Chris nods, and their foreheads touch as Caleb presses one finger inside. Chris sucks in a breath, and Caleb stills for a minute before pushing further. He doesn't know how long it's been since Chris did this, but he knows it's been at least a month, unless they've been doing it behind his back.

"I'm fine," Chris grunts. Caleb tries not to jump at his voice. Chris talks during sex. He knows this. Why the fuck did he think Chris would stop just because this is different? Probably because Chris has been silent since Scott pushed him over.

"Yeah?" Now it's a challenge. Now he wants to make Chris make noise again. He pushes in deeper, searching until he finds what he's looking for, and Chris groans.

"Fuck. Yeah. There." Chris melts against him, and somehow it's even hotter than Caleb thought it would be. He rubs again, and Chris squirms against him and fucking *whimpers*.

Then he freezes before Caleb can enjoy it. Dammit.

"Trust him." Scott says it low in Chris's ear, but Caleb can just make it out. Chris opens his eyes, and they stare at each other for a moment until Caleb nods, willing Chris to do it, trust him. Caleb doesn't realize he's holding his breath until Chris nods back and lets his head drop on Caleb's shoulder.

Caleb rubs inside of him again, and this time he doesn't hold back. He whines and pushes back on Caleb's finger until Scott pulls Caleb's hand away. Caleb wipes his hand off on Scott's thigh because whatever, Scott deserves it for walking them into this and not warning him that Chris was going to freak out.

He lets his hand wander up Chris's side as Scott pushes in and Chris moans into his neck, his long hair falling over his face and brushing against Caleb's neck. Caleb trails up Chris's neck with his thumb and pushes Chris's hair behind his ear. When Chris looks up, Caleb kisses him hard, fucking into his mouth as he reaches down and takes both of their cocks in his hand, pulling hard in time with Scott's thrusts.

"Fuck. Caleb." Chris pulls away from the kiss, and his fingers dig into Caleb's hip as his breaths get shorter.

61

"We got you. Come on," Caleb says, pulling hard and fast until Chris spills over his hand and slumps into his chest. The hot come over his cock brings him over after Chris, shuddering against Chris's lax body.

He's not sure when Scott finishes. He just feels Chris sigh as Scott pulls out. Scott better not think he's moving. No, Scott has to be the one that gets up.

Scott must know because he doesn't comment, just kisses Chris's shoulder before he gets out of bed and walks to the bathroom. When he comes back with a towel, he doesn't wipe them down like he usually does. Instead, he hands the towel to Chris to clean himself off and then Caleb. Chris tosses the towel back to Scott when he's finished and nudges Caleb's side.

"This doesn't mean you get to sleep in my spot," Chris says. His eyes have that fear in them again that Caleb doesn't like.

"Well, you're in my spot," Caleb says, but he laughs as the mood shifts back to normal, climbing over Chris as Chris shifts to the side. He stops halfway and lies on Chris's chest, letting his fingers trace over the mark he left there.

"You make your point?"

"Not exactly how I planned it."

"You could have just asked."

Caleb snorts. "Yeah, because we do heart to hearts so fucking well."

"True. That's what we have Scott for."

CHAPTER 8

CHRIS says they have to go out to celebrate, and he doesn't give a shit when Caleb points out that he really needs to get his shit together. Dan said they wanted him in three days which means he has to fly out in two. So he only has tonight and tomorrow before he has to get on a plane.

But Chris doesn't give a shit, and Scott promises to help him get things in order before he leaves, so he ends up in a bar when he should be packing. Danielle hugs him as soon as she sees him, but Jason hangs back until Chris and Scott leave him to get drinks from the bar. Jason smirks and nods to the hickeys Caleb knows are all too obvious on his neck.

"This isn't one of those times I can say 'you should see the other guy', is it?"

"Just saw the other guy, or guys. Not used to seeing Chris like that." Jason's right. It's always Scott who shows up with hickeys and bite marks.

Caleb shrugs, and he can't help the smirk he tries to hold back. "New rules."

"Good to know." Jason laughs and makes a show of keeping his distance as he pats Caleb on the shoulder. "Congrats on booking fashion week or whatever."

"Asshole." Caleb laughs as he pulls Jason into a hug, but he'd be lying if he said he didn't pull away a little sooner than he used to. If Chris wants some things for just himself and Scott, that's fair. He doesn't want to share them so much, either.

"So when do you leave?" Danielle asks as she takes the glass Scott hands her and leads them all to a table. He waits until they sit and then takes the seat in the middle of the three empty ones without thinking.

"Day after tomorrow."

"So we should all say goodbye to you tonight because you'll spend all of tomorrow in bed?" she giggles as Jason groans.

"Well, we were trying to be a little more subtle by calling you all and bringing him out tonight," Chris says as he sets a beer in front of Caleb, leaving an arm around the back of Caleb's chair when he sits down. Scott sits on his other side and lets his hand brush against Caleb's on the table when the guys groan again.

"I'm not drunk enough for this conversation," Jason says, waving to the waitress so he can order a round of tequila.

℘ℭ

SCOTT'S watching him when Caleb wakes up the morning he has to leave. Chris is still asleep, pressed close against his back.

"Hey." He has to remind himself that he wants this job. He doesn't want to spend a season out of work, but it's kind of hard with Chris's arm across his chest and Scott's hand rubbing over his hip.

"Hey. You've got about an hour before you have to leave," Scott says. "I got up and packed for you earlier. I can send more stuff later if you need it."

64

"Thanks." He's not sure when he collected so much stuff at Scott's place that it's enough to go to New York with. He doesn't know yet when he'll get time off, but he can't help hoping it's before he needs to call Scott for more things.

"Figured I'd let you sleep. We didn't let you get much last night."

"Wasn't complaining but thanks." Caleb pushes Scott's hair back from his face and leaves his hand at the back of Scott's neck to pull him into a kiss. "You'll check on my place? Drive my car enough that the oil doesn't settle if they don't give me time right away?"

"Yeah."

"We should get up," Caleb says, even though he really doesn't want to.

"You want breakfast?"

"Too early. I'll get something at the airport."

"Then we can stay in bed a while. We just have to get up and get dressed," Scott says, and he moves closer on the bed and lets his fingers run through Caleb's hair as they kiss. Caleb feels Chris's arm tighten around him before Chris says anything. Chris always holds him tighter just as he finds consciousness.

"Startin' something without me?" he says, and Caleb turns over on his back.

"Just waiting for you to wake up." He combs Chris's hair down with his fingers so it doesn't stick out in odd tangles. Chris kisses him, long and lazy, and when he breaks away, he turns into Chris's chest, pulling Scott's hand so Scott has to spoon close behind him. Chris doesn't say anything, just holds him tight between them a few seconds before Caleb feels them shift and opens his eyes to watch them kiss above him. When they pull back and settle on the bed around him, Caleb sighs and wishes he could fall back asleep just like this, even though he knows it would get uncomfortable in just a few minutes.

"They'll give you time off, and you'll be back in a couple weeks, at least. They'll probably give you your schedule in just a couple days, and we can book it." Scott kisses the back of his neck.

"Yeah," Caleb agrees, but Chris doesn't say anything. He just squeezes his arms around Caleb and rubs Caleb's back until Scott says they really do have to get up.

They dress without saying much, but he doesn't miss the ways Chris finds to brush against him and reach around him. They load his stuff into Scott's car, and Scott stops him before he gets in.

"Can't do this at the airport." Scott leans in to kiss him, letting his tongue rub against Caleb's. Caleb kisses back until he knows he needs to pull away or he's going to say fuck Fashion Week, he'd rather fuck Scott. Chris reaches for him then, and it's the opposite from normal. Where Scott kissed him hard, Chris kisses him slow, running his thumb over the side of Caleb's neck as he does.

They don't bother with small talk on the way to the airport, and he really hates that they can't go in with him.

"We should just say goodbye here. I'll be back in a couple weeks anyway," Caleb says. He sure as hell doesn't want to hug them in an airport and pretend they're just friends.

"Yeah," Scott agrees, leaning over to kiss him. "Don't forget to get something to eat before you get on the plane."

"Yeah, sure, Mom." Caleb rolls his eyes and gets out of the car so he can climb into the backseat with Chris. He tries to make the kiss quick, but Chris holds him in and lingers, kissing him again before letting him go.

"Call when you get there. Scott worries."

CHAPTER 9

THE first morning in New York, Caleb rolls over when he wakes, reaching for Chris on his left only to find empty space. Right. He's in New York and Chris and Scott are in LA. If he wants breakfast, he has to call room service or go downstairs. Either way, it's not going to be Scott's cooking.

He's awake before his wake-up call thanks to the flimsy hotel curtains, but not by much. He has just enough time to shower and sort through the suitcase of clothes he didn't pack. His fingers slide across glossy paper as he digs out a shirt and he pulls out a picture. It's old, from one of the first shows he went to. It might have been the first time he saw them play *together*. Either way, it was before things changed with them. But it's one of the only pictures they've taken all together. Caleb flips it over, but there's nothing written on the back except a date. He puts it in the drawer of the bedside table before he leaves.

It's been over a year since he moved out of New York, but Caleb still remembers how to take the subway to the apartment complex where he used to live. Nothing has changed except the doorman, who makes him call upstairs.

Jessie shrieks when she sees him, jumping into his arms and wrapping her legs around his waist while the doorman shifts his eyes away from the spectacle. Her brown, curly hair tickles his neck, and he's glad she's tiny enough that she can't topple him over.

"I didn't think I'd see you until tonight! Did you even check in at the office, yet?" Jessie asks as she hops down and pulls him to the elevator. For being less than five feet and probably only a hundred pounds, Jessie has always had an amazing ability to pull him wherever she wants.

"Not yet. I can only stay about an hour, and then I'll take the subway from here."

"An hour?" Jessie gives him a look as they step out of the elevator and walk toward the apartment they used to share. "Not that I didn't want to see you, but why didn't you just come over later?"

"I kind of need some help before I go to the office." Caleb slips off his jacket when they're inside. There's no way she can miss the two bruises Chris left high on his neck.

"Damn. Are you dating a vacuum cleaner?" She ignores his blush and pulls his shirt to the side so she can get a better look.

"So, is this one of those things you'd like me to cover up so well no one else knows about it?" Jessie asks as she leads him to a chair in front of the breakfast bar.

"I'd really appreciate it."

"Please tell me this is because you don't want anyone to know in general and not because I'm helping you cheat on someone. You haven't said anything about anyone since Damian left." Jessie says as she brings her giant makeup case in from another room and sets it on the counter. "Damn. If you're cheating, someone wants you to get caught."

"I'm not."

"So who's the lucky guy?" Jessie smirks, hopping onto the stool next to him as she opens drawers and pulls up trays.

Caleb shrugs. "It's new. Can we drop it for now?"

"You didn't seriously think I wasn't going to ask when I saw this." Jessie tests a few shades on his neck before picking a bottle.

"I didn't know I was coming here until a few days ago."

"Right. You thought you could just avoid the subject every time I called, and I'd never figure it out. Whatever. You know it's going to start to drive you crazy and you're going to blurt it all out." Jessie starts dabbing makeup on his neck, holding his head still as she works. "Are there more I'm going to have to cover up when you get a different shirt tomorrow?"

"Just this," Caleb sighs and pulls his collar down again.

"Wow. Okay. When you decide to tell me, I'm going to make you go back and tell this story." Jessie finishes her work on his neck and hands him a mirror. "What do you think?"

"I think you just saved my relationship." Caleb laughs. He can't see even a shade of a bruise.

"You said no cheating." Jessie eyes him like he just tricked her into being an accomplice to murder.

"I just meant now I don't have to get as mad that he did this to me." Not that Chris is completely off the hook, but maybe he'll forgive Scott.

"Okay, because for the record, I really wouldn't approve of that. But, yes, I know. I'm amazing." Jessie grins as she starts packing up her makeup. "And I expect you to come back after your meeting. You owe me dinner or something."

ℰↃCʒ

"HEY. How'd the first day go?" Chris asks when he answers the phone. Caleb really dialed Scott, but he's not surprised.

"My friend Jessie thinks I'm a freak because of you." Caleb says, but he's having a hard time staying mad. It's easier to be mad at Chris when he doesn't miss him.

"Aww, come on, darlin', you weren't exactly fighting me off."

"Not the point."

"So is this Jessie a guy?" Chris asks.

"Jessie is a girl. Short for Jessica." Caleb laughs. "Not very subtle, dude."

"I don't really do subtle." Chris laughs into the phone and Caleb really wishes he could shut him up in person—and maybe get a little revenge. "Have I heard of Jessie before?"

"I don't know. We were roommates when we interned at *TeenChic.* I might have mentioned her. Either way, if we were gonna fuck, we probably would've gotten drunk and done it years ago."

"That doesn't help me."

"I don't have sex with girls," Caleb says even though Chris *knows* this.

"They give you a schedule yet?" Chris asks, moving on like he's not going to go through Caleb's Myspace until he finds her.

"Yeah. I'm packed for about a week and half, but then I can actually fly back for almost a week."

"Yeah? Not bad." It would be better if he could see Chris's face, know if he's smiling like Caleb imagines.

"I figured Scott might miss me," Caleb says, and Chris actually laughs instead of just pretending they're really talking about Scott.

"Yeah. Scott misses you."

"I think I can speak for myself," Scott says as he comes on the line. "Can I assume Chris's mood shift means you're coming home soon?"

"Fuck off," he hears Chris mumble in the background.

"Yeah. Eight days here, and I'll be back for six." Caleb says.

"Sounds good. E-mail me your flight when you figure it out. Chris'll lose it and have to call you the day before."

"You still get picked up every time," Chris says. Caleb can hear the rustle of clothes as they settle together, on the couch, or the bed. He's not sure and asking would probably sound pathetic, but he can't forget that they're in LA together, and he's in New York by himself.

"Caleb? You still there?" Scott asks when he doesn't answer right away.

"Yeah, yeah. I'm here. I'll figure it out and e-mail you tomorrow." It's only eight days, but he's never left them alone for more than a day since he let Scott pull him into their bed. He can already tell he's not going to get any sleep thinking about what they might be doing while he's in New York.

ℬଔ

CALEB'S just finished shooting the reality show designer fitting one of her models when Scott calls the next day.

"Hey."

"Hey. Are you busy?" Scott asks. Caleb can't help smiling at his voice even though it earns him a curious glance from the model.

"No. I'm just packing up. Jessie's coming by so she doesn't get stuck going to a lunch with this girl she hates. Plus, I have to be

71

here early tomorrow, so I need to talk her into coming over in the morning again so she can re-cover all the hickeys."

"Sorry." Scott says, and Caleb can't hold it against him when he laughs. "If it helps, Danielle's still making fun of Chris."

"Doesn't hurt." Caleb laughs, but when Scott doesn't answer the silence isn't comfortable. "Still there?"

"Yeah. I'm here," Scott chuckles, but it's less than usual. "It's just... are you okay over there?"

"Me? Yeah, I'm fine."

"You didn't sound fine last night," Scott insists and he thinks there's a reason he and Chris tell Scott he's the girl. If it was up to them, they'd never talk about anything—which is probably why they need Scott.

"It was just a long day, and I'm still feeling the jet lag," Caleb says, hoping Scott won't catch the lie over the phone.

"You know we miss you, right? I mean, you know Chris isn't going to say it, but he was bitching all morning after he woke up alone. He acted like I don't get up two hours before him every day."

"I know. I'm fine." Caleb means it a little more this time. It's good to know he's not the only one who hates waking up alone, even if he is the only one falling asleep alone.

"Would you tell us if you weren't?" Scott asks and Caleb almost says his name, but he stops when Jessie comes in the door, waving as she walks over to him. Letting her hear Scott's name is just going to make her ask more questions. "So that's a no. You realize I have years of dealing with Chris, and I'll figure out a way to get it out of you."

"It's no big deal."

"If I don't figure it out before you get back, it's only seven days until I can get it out of you in person."

"Really, it's not a big deal. It's just weird being here." He doesn't add, *without y'all*.

"It's more than that. But I can wait to pry it out of you when you're not at work. We'll call you tonight."

"Yeah." Caleb answers. He should hang up soon. Jessie's already watching him with a worried look.

"I miss you. We both miss you. Okay? We'll be here when you get back. Whatever's wrong, I'm going to figure it out and do something about it," Scott says. Caleb has to laugh at how sure he is.

"Yeah. I'll talk to you tonight." Caleb sighs as he hangs up, and when he looks up, Jessie's watching him out of the corner of her eye. "What? You have a comment. Just say it."

"It's not my business." Jessie shrugs, and Caleb doesn't know why he doesn't let it drop there. Maybe it's just that he doesn't know anyone else here anymore, and at least Jessie already knows something is going on, so it's not like he's telling anyone new.

"Yeah, but say it anyway."

"You didn't say 'I love you' or 'I miss you' or anything. And that was… whoever gave you all the hickeys, right?"

"Yeah," Caleb says even though Chris really did most of them. He's not about to explain that. "But I told you it's kind of a new thing. We just started a month ago, so…"

"You're into it enough to try long distance for a few weeks, but not really to the 'I love you' point? Damn, this was shitty timing."

"Kind of—but with this job? There's always going to be traveling. He knew it could be like this from the beginning."

"You've got some time off after this week. Going home?"

"Yeah." Caleb smiles. Chris didn't even pretend not to be excited.

73

"Well, you're already planning that, and you're calling each other whenever you want instead of playing games, so I think you've got a good shot."

"In your professional opinion?" Caleb says, but he finds himself grinning at the vote of confidence anyway.

"Hey. You think you're the only guy I've had inside info on? I work with models. Yours aren't the first hickeys I've covered. I know shit."

CHAPTER 10

CHRIS calls after Jessie ditches him for her boyfriend, promising that she'll be back early in the morning. Caleb expects it to be both of them calling, but when he asks, Chris says he's driving to his own place for a while because Scott's got shit to do for a couple more hours. Caleb doesn't bother pointing out that it's the first time Chris has been to his apartment in five days.

"Why? I'm too boring for you without Scott? I'm offended," Chris says.

"No, you aren't."

"Not really. So what're you doing?"

"Just got back to the hotel, had an early morning, so I finished early." Caleb lies down on the bed. It's too big for just him.

"Scott's worried about you," Chris says.

"I'm fine." Caleb sighs. He'd rather deal with Chris not liking that he's hanging around models or something else that's easy. Chris doesn't argue, but he doesn't agree either. Caleb waits, listening to Chris breathe until he sighs. "Man, I don't want to talk about my feelings either. Change the subject."

"Oh thank god. Though I think Scott plans to make you later," Chris says. "Not that you can't with me. If you wanted to."

"I know. But I don't. I don't even want to talk about it with Scott."

"You know that tells me that there is something wrong, right?"

"I thought we were changing the subject," Caleb groans.

"We are. But just so you know, Scott isn't going to give up until he gets it out of you. He's like that."

"He'd have to be with you."

"What?" Chris asks, but he laughs. "Okay, that's fair. So doing anything interesting tonight?"

"I have to meet the designer tomorrow morning at seven."

"I'm so happy I'm unemployed."

❧

"HEY. Chris said he called you earlier too," Scott says when Caleb calls later that night.

"Yeah."

"He's on his way over here now. He's supposed to stop and get food. I'm kind of worried." Scott laughs because Chris likes to experiment with restaurants and sometimes this means they have to order pizza later.

"Good luck."

"Be happy you have room service," Scott laughs.

"Yeah," Caleb sighs.

"So how about you tell me what's going on?" Scott doesn't ease into it. He knows it will be easier without Chris around.

"Scott."

"Don't give me that, 'it's nothing' bullshit. I'm not going to buy it, and I really can't make a lot of guesses over the phone. It's hard to read you when you're not here." When he doesn't answer, Scott sighs. "Caleb, this distance thing sucks. It's going to be a lot harder if whenever you've got something going on, you make me wait until you're down here to get it out of you. You'll just be up there sitting on it for a week and upset for no reason."

"It's stupid." It's stupid, and it's not going to do any good to tell Scott anyway. Caleb's already decided that he's not going to ask them to take some kind of vow of celibacy while he's gone. They've been fucking a long time. They sleep in the same bed. They'll have sex when they want to have sex.

"I really doubt it, but if it is, you think I care? I've been with Chris off and on for four years. I really doubt you'll top his shit. The man had a quarter-life crisis when he turned twenty-five and did all kinds of stupid stuff to prove he wasn't old."

Caleb laughs. It's not fair that he didn't get to be around for that. "That's really not the issue."

"I'd hope not or you're a bit behind."

"No. Maybe when I hit thirty."

"So? Out with it," Scott says, and he doesn't even sound impatient yet.

"I think you're breaking up." Maybe he can crinkle some paper and blow into the phone and by tomorrow, Scott will have forgotten.

"I'll call the hotel and have them connect me to your room."

"That's a little insane."

"I have years of practice getting shit out of Chris. Give in while we still have time to have phone sex after we get this figured out."

"You have plans for phone sex?" Caleb thinks maybe he can distract Scott until he realizes he's not even sure how phone sex works with them. Do they wait until Chris gets there? Does he really want to get them all worked up so they can have sex later without him?

"I was hoping. You know Chris was. He starts to bitch after he's deprived for more than three days. He's having withdrawals from your ass."

"He's got your ass." Caleb says before he thinks better.

Scott doesn't answer him right away, and he really wants to take it back. "Is that not okay with you anymore?"

"It's fine."

"You don't sound fine. Do you not want to share Chris anymore?" Scott's question is quiet, and it takes Caleb too long to really understand what he's asking.

"No, Scott. No. I didn't mean that. Really. I like... I like how things are. I wouldn't do that to you." This is why Caleb doesn't talk about shit. It always comes out wrong.

"Caleb."

"Scott. Really. I mean it. You think I'm crazy? I don't want Chris to myself. We'd drive each other insane in a week and I'd never pick between y'all anyway. That's really not what I was thinking."

"Okay," Scott sighs, and Caleb really, really hates that he's not there. Now he's got to give Scott something.

"It's just weird with me here and y'all there—together."

"I know. I know it's weird. Things just don't feel right without you here."

"Thanks, but that's not really what I meant."

"What *did* you mean?" Scott asks. He doesn't press when Caleb doesn't answer right away, just waits until Caleb can figure out how to speak.

"I mean, I'm going to be gone a lot right now and y'all are both in LA. I know I can't expect for y'all to just wait for me to get home."

"I'm missing something, right? Because we already said we'd make this work."

"I meant…." Fuck. What is he? A dumb teenager who can't say the word *sex* without blushing? "I meant I know I can't expect you to not fuck until I'm home, but it's weird to think about."

Caleb doesn't realize until he says it and Scott doesn't answer right away that it's more than weird. He really doesn't like the idea at all. It's not like he'd fuck Scott without Chris there.

"Caleb. We don't fuck when you aren't here. You really thought we would?"

"You don't? You never said anything. And I'm not just going to be at my place for a night. I'm gone for a week."

"We wouldn't do that without talking to you—which I probably should have done, because we know Chris wasn't going to do it. But I'm telling you, we don't. Are you fucking Chris while I'm not around?"

"No! But—"

"No. It's us three. Caleb, come on. We've said that. I'm going to let Chris tattoo it on your ass. Not me and Chris together and you on the side. When you're not here, we kiss, we sleep in the same bed, and sometimes we jack off together. That's it," Scott says like it's insane that he thought otherwise.

"Really?"

"You're right. It was stupid. You should have just asked a long time ago. We're not teenagers. We can control ourselves."

"Shut up," Caleb says, but he can't help laughing. "I didn't want to tell you guys what to do."

"We thought it was obvious. But if it's not, for the record, you and Chris can't fuck if I'm not there unless I'm on the phone telling you what to do to each other. And then it probably won't be fucking."

"So that's how phone sex works? I get to call the shots."

"Sure. I hadn't really had long brooding thoughts about it." Scott laughs. It's unfair Caleb can't shut him up the way he wants to. Before he comes up with an answer, he hears a door slam closed over the line.

"Is all the girly sharing of feelings over? Because I took as long as I could to get over here."

"Please tell me the next time you make him talk you'll tape it for me," Caleb says, because damn, it has to happen sometimes.

"I think he'd kill us both." Scott's laugh is muffled and he hears them kiss over the phone.

"So, darlin', is everything really okay?" Chris asks.

"Yeah, yeah. We're good," Caleb says. Scott will probably tell Chris later, but that's fine because Chris won't ever say anything about it.

"Good, because we really haven't been having enough fun on the phone."

Caleb laughs. "Is this really all y'all do when you're away from each other?"

"It doesn't work for you?" Chris asks and Caleb can see Chris's frown in his mind.

"No. It's cool," Caleb says and Chris starts laughing. Asshole. Caleb can't even hit him right now.

"You've never done this?"

"I've done it. I just don't fucking plan it. I let it happen naturally."

"Sorry. I didn't realize I had to get you in the mood." Chris is still laughing as he hears them fighting for the phone.

"Stop being an asshole. I'm kicking your ass and jacking off in the shower alone if he hangs up." Scott's comment to Chris is muffled before he talks into the phone. "How about we move to the bedroom, put the phone on speaker and you can tell me what you want me to do. Or we can keep the phone off speaker and you can tell me what to do to Chris and leave him in the dark until he stops pissing us off."

"So pretty much forever."

Scott laughs and Caleb's not surprised to hear Chris bitching in the background, but he can hear the bedroom door creak open and slam closed.

"So what're you wearing?" Scott asks, laughing and Caleb relaxes.

"Sweatpants and a T-shirt."

"Get rid of the T-shirt."

"Both of you too," Caleb says before he puts down the phone to pull off his shirt.

"Chris was already shirtless. Man doesn't wait for directions for shit."

"That's shocking."

"So how do you want us?" Scott asks and Caleb lets his eyes slide closed to block out his banal hotel room. He thinks of the soft brown tones of Scott's room, with the old shag carpet Caleb makes fun of and the comforter Scott's probably had since he moved out of his parents' house.

"Chris on his back on the bed."

"Okay," Scott says to Caleb, and then, "On your back," to Chris.

"Put it on speaker. I want to hear him while you suck him off," Caleb says, because he knows they both must miss it if they haven't been doing it since he left.

"You gonna let him in on the plan?" Scott says.

"We'll let him figure it out. Take your time getting there." Caleb knows Scott's not going to be able to tease much, but it's worth a try. Chris wasn't lying when he first told Caleb that Scott was a cockslut. The line fuzzes as Scott switches it to speaker.

"Hey, darlin'. You decided I get to talk now?"

"Wanted to hear you while he gets you off."

"Tell me where you are. Are you naked? On the bed?" Chris asks.

"On the bed. Still have sweatpants on."

"No underwear?"

"I was planning to sleep after I called," Caleb says.

"Hum… take the pants off. Want to think of you naked," Chris says before he moans long and low.

"Like something as minor as me wearing clothes has ever stopped you," Caleb answers, but he pushes off the sweatpants anyway. "Tell me what Scott's doing to you."

"Teasing. Like I'm sure you told him to do. Sucking everywhere but my cock."

"Fuck." Caleb reaches down, wraps a fist around his already hard cock.

"That work for you? You know how fucking hot he looks when he's trying to hold back, but you know he wants it. Fuck!" Chris gasps and moans as Caleb pulls on his own cock again. "Fuck. He's just sucking my balls, got them in his mouth."

Caleb moans into the phone, thinking of Scott sucking him off.

"Jacking yourself now?" Chris asks. "Pretending it's me?"

"Pretending it's Scott," Caleb says, even though his mind shifts to Chris as soon as Chris asks.

"Yeah, sure. I know you like it when I jack you off. I know you like it hard and fast. You try to hold back and you know that makes me just want to make you come even more. You like it when I lick up your balls, and you have to grab onto something not to lose it."

Caleb moans and decides it doesn't matter if he comes too quickly listening to Chris's voice. He can just lie about it. Not that Chris will believe him; he's obviously had too much practice at this.

"Heard that. Stop holding back. Oh fuck!" Chris moans and Caleb can hear him panting. "Fuck, his mouth is hot. You know he fucking loves it. Loves having my cock in his mouth. Loves having *your* cock in his mouth. You know he misses it. Misses it in his mouth, misses your cock in his ass. Fuck, I miss watching him with you."

"Fuck. Chris." It's all Caleb can manage as he hears Chris's breaths get shorter.

"Come on, darlin'. Scott's getting there. Started jacking himself off as soon as I mentioned your cock."

"And you? Wanna hear you."

"Yeah. Fuck." Chris pants and gasps as he comes. Caleb thinks about him, hand in Scott's hair as he comes in Scott's mouth.

"Like that?" Scott asks, mouth empty again.

"Yeah. I'm close."

"He's right. I miss your cock. He does too. Just hasn't had the balls to ask you to fuck him yet," Scott says, and he's pretty sure Chris bitches after it, but Caleb's brain is too busy coming for him to give a shit. Scott knows what Chris wants better than Chris anyway.

"Can't wait to see that," Scott breathes into the phone and goes quiet.

"Think y'all are the ones wanting that. Seeing how you both lost it as soon as you thought about it," Chris says. Caleb's pretty sure he's rolling his eyes.

"Whatever. You know you want it," Scott laughs.

Caleb tries to answer but only manages a sigh. It's been a long day and sex always makes him tired.

"Think you'll sleep better tonight, darlin'?"

"Um hum."

"Good. Just six days, babe. Hang up the phone before you fall asleep with it on."

℘℃

"FLYING home tomorrow?" Jessie asks as she brushes powder over his neck. The hickeys are almost faded now.

"Yeah," Caleb says and even though he tries to hold it back, a smile slips onto his face.

"Stop trying to play it off. I need someone to live through."

"Why?" Jessie had a boyfriend last time he checked.

"I'm starting to think Drake's gay. He won't go past third base. When I heard that you were going to be in town, I was going to make you hit on him and see what happened. Then I saw you and found out you have a possessive freak for a boyfriend."

"I wish I could say he wasn't that bad, but he sort of is."

"As long as he's not creepy and abusive about it."

Caleb shakes his head, and she glares and holds him still so she can finish.

84

His phone buzzes on the counter and Jessie frowns. "Don't move. I'll get it for you. You're killing my vision with all your fucking moving."

"Sorry, you know it doesn't have to be perfect. They're almost gone anyway." Caleb laughs as she reaches behind him, picks his phone up from the table and hands it to him. "It's a text. It vibrates for a text. I can't look unless you let me move."

"Yeah, yeah. I know. It's probably your boyfriend, or whatever, who texts you twenty times a day. You can wait until I finish. It sort of does have to be perfect if you don't want people to figure out that you have makeup on." Jessie stands back and surveys her work.

"He doesn't text that much," Caleb says, even though they do text that much because it's not like she's there to notice all of them. He's pretty sure it's some plot Scott came up with to make sure he knows they won't forget about him. Sometimes they do get up to ten texts each a day. More if he has a break in the day to answer.

"It totally is and you know it," Jessie says, and then he sighs when he smiles again. "Okay, just read it. Every time you think about it, you smile and it distracts me with how sappy and cute you are and I can't do the makeup anyway."

"You could just leave it," Caleb says just to piss her off as he looks at the phone. It's Chris. *Jason called. I told him you might find time to hang out on Tuesday, but you wouldn't be able to sit down.*

"You say that now. When one of your models asks why her photographer is wearing makeup, you'll be pissed. Can you keep a straight face so I can finish now?"

"Bitch," Caleb laughs and then shifts into a straight face so she can finish.

"You love me, which is why you're not going to come back with five new hickeys for me to cover up. I like hanging out with you, but I'm making you restock my makeup supply if this continues."

CHAPTER 11

CHRIS sees Caleb first when he walks into the crowded baggage claim of LAX, dragging his carry-on behind him. He elbows Scott and gets up, trying not to smile as he walks toward Caleb, but he fails, breaking into a smile and shrugging before pulling Caleb into his arms. Caleb lets his face rest against Chris's neck and breathes in: shampoo, just a hint of cigarette smoke, and *Chris*.

"That's all you brought?" Chris asks as he pulls back and gives Scott a turn.

"I've still got lots of stuff at my apartment, and Jessie let me leave some of my stuff at her place. It's easier to move it from her apartment to the hotel than to bring it all back here," Caleb says instead of admitting that he really didn't want to be stuck at the airport any longer than he had to.

"Yeah," Chris says, throwing an arm over his shoulders and leaning close as he leads them out of the airport. "And you don't need a lot of clothes anyway."

Caleb groans, and he's trying to lean closer when Scott pulls him away from Chris and pushes him toward the front seat of the car. "You sit in the front. I'm not crashing the car because you two can't make it all the way home."

"Ass. You just want him up front where you can feel him up while you're driving." Chris climbs in the back anyway as Scott throws Caleb's bag into the trunk and walks around to the driver's side.

They both reach for him as soon as the car doors close and he's really not sure who's moaning as two tongues push into his mouth. Two hands clutch at the back of his neck, holding him in as they kiss hard and desperate. When he finally breaks away, he lets their foreheads rest together as they catch their breath. It has to be uncomfortable for Chris, leaning into the front seat like he is, but he pulls them into another three-way kiss anyway, sliding his tongue between them both.

"Fuck. We gotta stop so we can get home," Scott says when they pull back the second time.

"You drive. We'll make out," Chris says. He tries to pull Caleb toward him, but Scott pushes him back in his seat.

"You're not making me crash because you can't keep your hands off him," Scott says. He holds Chris back until he slides into his seat and buckles up, bitching the entire time.

Scott laughs, and Caleb's really not sure what the point is anyway. Scott's hand runs over his thigh as he drives, and Chris leans forward, hands feeling over his chest as he licks the shell of Caleb's ear.

"Gonna let you fuck me when we get home," Chris whispers in his ear, and a moan slips past Caleb's lips before he can stop himself. "Gonna let you fuck me hard, because I like it rough. Been thinking of you bending me over the couch while Scott sucks me off."

"I don't even need to ask what he's saying to you," Scott says when Caleb moans again and shifts in his seat. He's hard already, and Chris has his arms pinned down so he can't even reach back and touch him.

"You could help me," Caleb says, sucking in a breath as Chris bites his ear.

"Help you how? You don't really want him to stop." Scott laughs as Caleb squirms under Chris's hands and tongue.

"You know you like it," Chris breathes in his ear again. "You're thinking about fucking me, holding me down, pulling my hair. You've been thinking about it since Scott brought it up, probably since you watched Scott fuck me. You wanna get your hands in Scott's hair while he sucks me off. You like watching him with cock in his mouth as much as I do."

"Fuck," Caleb can't help bucking his hips as Scott's hand travels up his thigh. He stops just short of Caleb's cock. Bastard.

"Can't have you coming before we even get home," Chris says loud enough for Scott to hear this time, and they both chuckle.

"That's true. Because he's only going to give it up this easy once. After that, he's going to make you work for it," Scott says, but he moves his hand up anyway, pressing down on Caleb's cock.

"Yeah. And you better enjoy it. I don't bend over just because you ask. Not that I don't know Scott will give you tips. Maybe if you're nice, he'll tell you his tricks, because it's taken him a few years to get them down," Chris is whispering again, breath hot in Caleb's ear as he rubs over Caleb's chest. Caleb pushes into Scott's hand again and leans his head back. "And he's the only one that can help you. Never let anyone fuck me before except him. Just gonna be you and him."

Caleb tries to turn his head now, tries to see Chris, but Chris moves when he does and Caleb gets the point. He faces forward again and laces his fingers with Chris's hand, pulling until Chris comes back, kissing down Caleb's neck. Caleb moans and lets his eyes slip closed as Chris mouths under his shirt.

He doesn't open his eyes until the car stops and Scott kills the engine. Then he's fumbling with his seatbelt and getting out of the car. He pulls Chris to him as soon as he gets out, kissing him hard and holding him there with a hand on the back of Chris's neck. "Gonna fuck you so hard, and you're gonna love every second."

Chris moans as Scott pulls Caleb away and toward the house. Chris follows, and they push him against the back of the door as soon as it slams closed, kissing him hard and fighting for his lips. Just as he starts to worry they're going to actually fight, Chris breaks away and pushes up Caleb's shirt, kissing up his chest until Scott grabs the T-shirt and pulls it over his head. Scott finally breaks away, letting out a satisfied sigh against Caleb's cheek. "We might have missed you a little."

"Yeah." Caleb smiles, and Scott nods as Caleb reaches for Chris. Chris is really wearing too many clothes when he's supposed to be getting fucked. He kisses Chris long and slow even when Chris tries to make it rough. Chris can try all he wants. Caleb's calling the shots now. Chris tries to look away when Caleb pulls back, but Caleb holds him, making Chris look at him. "Hey. Don't be an idiot about this."

Chris nods and relaxes when Scott wraps his arms around him from behind, kissing his neck and reaching past him to pull Caleb with them as he backs them toward the couch. Chris turns around, stripping Scott's shirt from his body and pushing down his jeans. He threads his fingers through Scott's hair and kisses him, only letting go when Scott reaches up and strokes his thumb over Chris's cheek. Caleb's not sure what they're telling each other, but he feels the muscles in Chris's back relax before Scott sits down and starts working Chris's jeans open.

Caleb leans down, kissing Scott before he pushes Chris's shirt up and off. Scott chuckles and reaches back to slap Caleb's ass. "You need to catch up."

"It's not my fault you both forgot to get me naked," Caleb laughs as he pushes down his own jeans and kicks them away.

"Sorry," Scott smirks as he pulls on Chris's hips, bringing him close and sucking on his hip as Caleb presses against his back, kissing down his neck and rubbing over his chest. Chris sighs and leans back against Caleb's chest. Caleb can feel him trying to relax, but that's the problem. He's having to *try*.

Caleb doesn't say anything, just squeezes the hand Scott has on Chris's hip. Scott squeezes back and starts kissing up Chris's chest until he's standing again. He kisses Chris long and hard and then starts kissing down the side of his neck. Caleb takes the other side of Chris's neck, trapping Chris between them and rubbing over his back. Scott's whispering something in Chris's ear that he can't hear, and he wonders if Scott will tell him later if he asks. Chris finally sighs and leans against Scott, and he doesn't tense when Caleb reaches down and strokes his cock.

"I'm right here," Caleb hears Scott whisper when curiosity wins out and he kisses to the back of Chris's neck to try and hear something. He's not trying to eavesdrop; he just wants to make sure he's not screwing this up is all. "I've got you. Caleb's got you. Just let go."

Chris moans and fucks into Caleb's hand, making his ass rub against Caleb's cock. He pulls Scott's lips to his, kissing him hard, and then pushes him down. Scott smirks as he sits down, leaning forward to suck Chris into his mouth. Caleb can feel Scott's lips against his hand as Chris leans back against him.

"I'm good," Chris says even though he didn't ask, turning his head and reaching back to pull Caleb into a kiss.

"Yeah? How do you want it?"

"Like I said... hard. Like this," Chris sighs and Caleb's not sure where Scott found the lube he puts in Caleb's hand, but he's not surprised because he gets the idea that they planned this.

Chris moans as Caleb trails a finger down the cleft of his ass. Scott's still working him hard, and Caleb has to wrap an arm around Chris's waist to keep him from thrusting into Scott's mouth. Caleb sucks hard on Chris's shoulder and bites down just a little as he pushes a finger inside.

Chris sucks in a breath as Caleb pushes in further, mouthing at Chris's neck as he does. He's probably going to leave a mark, but Chris moans and pushes back anyway. It's not like Chris cares if he gets a little marked up.

"More. I can take more," Chris moans, leaning over Scott to grip the back of the couch, and Caleb rubs his hand over Chris's back as he pushes in a second finger. Chris gasps as he opens up and pushes back against Caleb's hand. "More."

"Getting there," Caleb whispers as he leans over Chris's back. Scott hands him a condom, and he has to pull both fingers out of Chris to roll it over his cock and slick himself with lube. He doesn't ask if Chris is ready, just presses the head of his cock against Chris's ass and pushes forward when Chris pushes back. He's not sure who moans. Maybe they all do, because when he pushes all the way in and leans over Chris, Scott has pulled back to watch.

Caleb waits, kissing and nipping at Chris's back until Chris grunts and reaches back to slap Caleb's ass. "Come on. I'm not gonna break."

Caleb bites back a laugh, sharing a look with Scott over Chris's shoulder before he starts to move and forgets about everything except how hot and tight Chris is. He moans, pressing his head between Chris's shoulders as he thrusts. When he opens his eyes, Scott is kissing Chris hard and fisting his own cock. Scott keeps a hand on Chris's cheek when he pulls back, watching Chris's face as Caleb reaches around to stroke Chris's cock.

Chris is close, his breaths coming short and fast. Caleb bites and nips at Chris's back as he thrusts, and Chris stills, spilling come over Caleb's hand and Scott's cock. When Caleb pulls back, he licks over the light teeth marks on Chris's skin.

"Fuck. Chris," Scott moans, rubbing hot come over his dick and coming hard. That's it for Caleb. He thrusts hard twice and squeezes hard on Chris's hip as he comes.

"I can't have both of you falling on me," Scott's saying when Caleb comes back into his head. Scott's hands are resting on Chris's hips, and Chris's arms are trembling just enough for Caleb to notice. Right. Chris probably shouldn't have to support his own weight plus Caleb on his back right after that. Standing up isn't easy, but somehow Caleb manages to do it as he pulls out and falls on the couch next to Scott. Chris sighs and starts to fall forward, but Scott pushes him toward Caleb, so he ends up straddling Caleb's lap instead.

"Just tired," Chris mumbles as his head falls on Caleb's shoulder. Scott cuddles against his side and reaches over to run a hand through Chris's hair and down his back. He nods at Caleb's confused look and smiles when Caleb wraps his arms around Chris's back, holding him tighter.

"Yeah, I know," Caleb agrees, kissing the top of his head and staying silent until Chris sighs and gets up.

They're all quiet as they slip past each other in the shower. Caleb's next place needs to have a huge shower, because it's not fair that only two of them can fit in the shower at once.

Caleb towels off and makes it into bed first, Chris climbing in after him and spooning against his back. Caleb tilts his head back for a kiss just as Scott climbs under the covers on his other side.

"S'good to have you back," Scott says, leaning over to kiss Chris and then lying down to kiss Caleb long and slow.

"Yeah," Caleb mumbles, already drifting off to sleep between the safe warmth of their bodies.

ᛯ

CHRIS is still asleep when Caleb wakes up the next morning. He's too used to those damn early morning shoots. At least the room isn't lit up already like it always is in New York, but it isn't too late, because there's still an indention where Scott's head had been on the pillow.

Chris is on his side, arm draped over Caleb's hip and Caleb turns, pushing Chris onto his back so he can drape over his chest. When Chris wakes, he can just say he must have moved in his sleep.

Caleb traces his hand over the muscles of Chris's chest, enjoying the warmth under him. It's always so cold in the morning in New York, and it doesn't help when Caleb rolls over onto the empty side of the bed next to him. The first four days in New York, he rolled over into that cold spot reaching for Chris and feeling his chest tighten when he remembered Chris was miles away.

Chris sighs as Caleb tangles a hand in his hair, and his arms come up to wrap around Caleb's waist. "Mornin'"

"Humm," Caleb mumbles, "Still early."

"Yeah," Chris whispers and warm hands stroke over Caleb's back. It's not *that* early, but he really doesn't want to get up. He wants to stay in bed all day and pretend he doesn't have to leave again in a few days.

"Do we have plans for today?" Caleb asks, because for all he knows Chris has studio time scheduled, and Scott has something else lined up. There's no way they can just shut down for five days.

"Um hum. Lots of stuff," Chris says, and Caleb feels the press of Chris's lips on his forehead as he sighs.

"So when do I have to get up?"

"Tomorrow, but you'll probably want to shower or take a piss at some point."

"What?"

93

"I said we had plans. Not that you had to get out of bed for them," Chris says as he lets one of his hands drift lower, rubbing over Caleb's ass.

"Asshole," Caleb laughs, but it changes to a gasp as Chris lets a finger slide between his cheeks to rub against him.

"That's just what I was thinking," Chris says, and Caleb really wants to call him on his stupid joke, but Chris is rubbing circles over his hole and it's distracting. Caleb's just thinking they need to get Scott when Chris yells, "Scott! Get in here."

"You're up early. I haven't even started—" Scott says and stops short when he sees them on the bed. "I should kill you for starting without me."

"Didn't really start. Just teasing," Chris says, rubbing harder as Scott lies down behind Caleb, but still not doing anything else.

"Yeah?" Scott's hand snakes around his waist, wrapping his hand around Caleb's cock and stroking him until he's hard and moaning into Chris's chest. Chris's finger leaves him and he can hear Chris fumbling with the drawer behind him as Caleb bucks into Scott's hand.

"You been missing me, darlin'?" Chris says as he pushes a lubed finger inside. Fuck, Caleb *did* miss this.

"I think you've been missing me more." He's really tempted to remind Chris that his cock was in Chris's ass just a few hours ago, but Chris pushes in deeper, rubbing inside him and he pushes into Chris's chest instead.

"Hey," Chris says to get his attention, and when he looks up Chris closes in on his mouth, kissing him long and rough as Scott mouths at his shoulder. When Chris pulls away, he nips at Caleb's bottom lip as he talks, "Turn around for me. I have been missing your ass."

"Yeah, so you told me everyday." Caleb mumbles, but he turns over to face Scott anyway.

Scott tastes like toothpaste and coffee when they kiss, and Caleb thinks that maybe it's not fair Scott's having to put up with their morning breath, but he wraps his arms around Scott's back and pulls him closer anyway.

"Hum. Where'd you want my mouth, babe?" Scott asks when he pulls back from the kiss.

"Everywhere," he says, and Scott chuckles.

"Can't be everywhere. And we're not adding a fourth."

"Fine," Caleb says before pushing Scott down toward his cock, because he likes kissing Scott, but Chris has two fingers in his ass, and he really likes Scott sucking his cock while he's getting fucked.

"You good?" Chris asks as he rubs over Caleb's prostate again, making his head swim as Scott licks down his chest.

"Yeah. I'm good."

Scott's lips close around his cock just as Chris pulls his fingers out and then the head of Chris's cock is pressing against him.

"You missed my cock?" Chris asks, still not pushing inside.

"You're a fucking tease."

"If you didn't, I could stop."

"Fine, I missed your cock. Fuck me already." He's pretty sure that he doesn't actually yell, but he does push back as Chris pushes inside, sliding in slowly until he's buried deep in Caleb's ass. Chris holds still for a moment as he takes a deep breath and reaches around Caleb to run a hand through Scott's hair.

"I'm good. Fucking move already," Caleb chokes out as Scott swirls his tongue over the head of Caleb's cock.

Chris finally fucking moves, holding tight to Caleb's hips to keep from pushing him too hard into Scott's mouth and fuck, this was why he hated being in New York. Scott's mouth is hot on his cock as Chris sucks and bites into his shoulder, thrusting quick and hard until all he can do is pull on Scott's hair to warn him before he's coming hard into Scott's mouth. Scott swallows, licking the last of the come from his cock before he licks back up Caleb's body to find his mouth, licking inside so Caleb can taste himself in Scott's mouth.

Caleb reaches for Scott's cock, jacking him off as he fucks Caleb's mouth with his tongue and Chris grunts just as Scott does, pushing hard into Caleb's ass and coming as Scott spills hot over their hands.

"Fuck." One of them says it, but Caleb isn't even sure which one.

"It's really, really my turn next," Scott mumbles into Caleb's neck. "We're just keeping you in the bed all fucking day."

CHAPTER 12

CHRIS is asleep when Caleb wakes up the second time, and he's pressed so close against Caleb's back, hot breath on the back of Caleb's neck, that he knows there's no way he can move without waking Chris up.

Scott's watching Caleb when he opens his eyes. Scott smiles as he runs a hand over Caleb's jaw as he wakes up.

"Hey," Scott says against his lips.

"Hey."

"Can you breathe with that death grip he's got on you?" Scott smiles and looks down at the arm Chris has across his chest.

"Just barely."

"He missed you a lot."

"Just him?"

"No. I missed you. You know that. I can just say it myself," Scott says, smiling as he moves closer and presses a kiss to Caleb's lips.

"Missed you too. Both of you," Caleb says. Scott moves closer and presses his face into Caleb's neck so Caleb can smell his shampoo. He reaches up, tangling his hands in Scott's hair and holding him close.

"Yeah," Scott sighs against him, and takes a deep breath as if he's trying to breathe Caleb in.

"Hey, you okay?" Caleb asks when Scott stays where he is and doesn't say anything.

"Yeah, fine." Scott edges back a little, but not enough for Caleb to see his face.

"Liar," Caleb says, running his hand through Scott's hair and leaning down to kiss his forehead.

"No. I'm fine now." Scott's not usually so hard to figure out, but he wonders if Chris and he let things slip because they assume Scott will tell them.

"But you weren't?"

"I was just worried you might not come back. You could get up there away from us, and realize this is weird and not normal, and you could find something normal." Scott shrugs, letting his head lean against Caleb's chest.

"What? No. Scott, no. I wouldn't just forget you. I'm still not going to forget you when I go back. You're the one who said we'd make this work."

"I know. I just, I know I will and I know Chris will because we're just so much better with you. We don't fight like we used to and he doesn't frustrate me like he used to. But...."

"I'm better with y'all too. I'm not over there looking for normal. I'm not going to forget about either of you. I'm sorry. It probably didn't help that you knew something was wrong and I didn't tell you right away. But I thought about you all the time. I thought you knew that." Caleb runs his fingers through Scott's hair again and pulls just enough to make Scott look up at him. "You know, Jessie makes fun of me because she says I smile every time you text me."

"Yeah?"

"Yeah. Then she hits me because she says it's distracting if I'm grinning like an idiot," he says as Chris's arm tightens against his chest. "Did Chris know about this?"

"No. He would've told you," Scott says and Caleb knows it's unfair to talk about this with Chris waking up behind him, but Chris should know, and Scott would let him tell Chris later anyway. It's just better if Chris hears it himself.

"Yeah, well, *you* should have told one of us so I could tell you there was no fucking way I was just going to find someone else in New York." Caleb leans forward to kiss Scott long and slow and feels the press of Chris's lips against his back.

When he pulls back, Scott is smiling and Chris's arm slides to Caleb's hip as Chris props himself up to look at Scott.

"Did I wake up just in time for the sex?"

"Your timing is too convenient," Scott says, but he laughs and pulls Caleb on top of him, letting his legs fall open so Caleb can settle between them. Caleb kisses Scott again, drawing it out as Chris watches them and runs a hand down Caleb's back. He'll never stop being shocked that not only does Chris allow this, but he also pushes the bottle of lube and a condom into Caleb's hand.

They don't talk as they open Scott up together. They just lick and kiss and watch as Scott sighs and moans. They all kiss as Caleb slides inside, tongues mixing together and swallowing moans.

"So fucking beautiful," Chris says, moving behind Caleb and licking down his spine as he fucks into Scott, slow and deep even as Scott whimpers and asks for more, harder. But Caleb knows he really likes it slow, pressed chest to chest while Caleb makes him wait. Caleb gasps in the middle of the kiss as Chris licks lower. Fuck, he's wanted this, but never managed to ask for it.

"You like that?" Chris asks and Caleb's pretty sure it's because he made some kind of almost-sobbing sound about the time Chris started licking down his crack, so he doesn't justify it with an answer. He just uses the break to get back to fucking Scott just like

99

he likes it. Having Chris's tongue licking him open makes it really fucking hard to keep his pace slow enough to drive Scott insane.

"Know you do." Chris starts to lean down again, but Scott reaches around Caleb and pulls on his arm until Chris gives in and lies down on his side facing them.

"Let him fuck me without you distracting him for once," Scott says. Caleb chuckles with Chris as he pulls out and pushes back slow enough to make Scott moan and pull Caleb closer so that they can kiss. He pulls out again and feels Chris's hand slip between them and grip Scott's cock, matching Caleb's thrusts with long slow pulls. Scott's turn to be the center of attention *is* a bit overdue.

"Better?" Chris asks when they break their kiss and Scott nods as Chris turns his head, pulling Scott into his own kiss and fuck, he could watch them kiss all day. He's the only one that gets to see them kiss like this, more obscene than they'll ever kiss in front of anyone else no matter how drunk they get.

Scott starts to push against him, reaching down to wrap a fist around Chris's cock and getting too desperate for the long slow fuck. He whines when Caleb rolls his hips instead of fucking him harder, but Caleb doesn't change his pace. He waits until Scott begs, hand tightening on Chris's cock and jerking hard, before he gives in and fucks Scott hard and fast, coming just after Scott pushes into Chris's hand and spills between them. Caleb falls on top of him for a moment before he comes back to himself and scrambles down the bed to suck Chris into his mouth. They're kissing when Chris comes, hot and thick on Caleb's tongue.

"We need food," Chris mumbles as Caleb crawls back up the bed between them.

"Yeah," Scott says, "You should work on that."

"*I* should work on it?" Chris smirks, his hand running through Scott's hair.

"You can cook. Stop making Caleb think you can't."

"You just don't want to get up because you're all fucked out."

"So? I should get breakfast in bed sometimes too." Scott rolls his eyes, pulling Caleb closer in his arms as Chris laughs.

"Fair enough. I'm only leaving Caleb with you because he'll make me burn something and we need energy to keep doing this."

ℰℐℂℛ

CHRIS *can* cook… that liar. But it's so good that Caleb can forgive him and he doesn't really mind helping Scott clean up in the kitchen while Chris showers.

Except that Chris takes long showers and they're finished before he is. It's really not their fault that they get bored and wander into the bathroom where Scott presses him against the counter to make out. Chris's body is blurred through the glass of the shower door, but it's enough for them to imagine and he knows Chris can see enough to figure out the show they're giving him.

"How long do think it'll take?" Scott whispers in his ear as he kisses up Caleb's neck.

"Less than a minute." It's not that he doesn't believe Chris has willpower; it's just that Chris isn't much for resisting things he wants without a damn good reason.

"Get up," Scott taps the counter, pushing against him until he gives in and jumps up to sit on the counter, letting his legs fall open for Scott to step between them.

"I can't get through a shower without a porno in my bathroom?" Chris says as he steps out of the shower and runs a towel over his hair. He steps behind Scott and his skin is still slick from the shower when Caleb reaches for him.

101

"You took too long," Caleb mumbles, letting his head fall back as Scott kisses down his neck. Chris trails a hand over his side and down one of the legs he has wrapped around Scott's waist.

"You don't usually mind me taking so long," Chris answers, and Scott chuckles against his chest.

"I do when it takes you this long to get started."

Chris rolls his eyes and reaches around him to get condoms and lube from the medicine cabinet. He's not so blind that he doesn't notice Chris has more than one.

"Dude, that isn't going to work." They've tried fucking like this before, except last time it was on the bed with Chris trying to fuck him while he fucked Scott. It was impossible to get a good rhythm and it was so awkward that the heat was gone and none of them even got off. And Caleb really wants to get off this time.

"You have no sense of adventure," Chris says, urging Scott to pull Caleb forward on the counter so Chris can ease a lubed finger inside. It hasn't been long, and Caleb can tell Chris is watching his face, looking for any sign he's too sore for this, even though Chris was just as careful the last time.

"I have a sense of adventure. I'm with *you*," Caleb manages even as Chris hits just the right spot.

"So funny." Chris smirks, ripping open a condom and rolling it over Scott's cock. Caleb gives up thinking of a comeback as Scott pushes inside Caleb.

"Good, baby?" Scott asks, kissing just behind his ear.

"Mm, yeah, I'm good." Caleb leans back and the edge of the mirror digs into his back, but the angle is better and it lets Scott fuck into him just right.

He can see it on Scott's face when Chris starts to stretch him open. Scott gasps and he thrusts into Caleb harder, fingers digging into Caleb's thighs.

"Caleb," Scott moans, mouth falling open as Chris pushes into him. It's always hot watching Scott while Chris fucks him, but this might just beat all the other times.

"Give me some space, darlin'," Chris drawls, easing Caleb's legs open so he can press fully against Scott's back with Caleb's legs wrapped around them both.

"One of you needs to fucking move," Caleb bites off the words and Chris chuckles and reaches around to grip his cock.

"Come on. Caleb wants it. I left you enough space," Chris says, mouthing up the side of Scott's neck and Scott loses it, fucking himself on Chris's cock as he fucks Caleb fast and hard, collapsing onto Caleb's chest as he comes. Chris takes over, fucking Scott against him and pulling on Caleb's cock until Caleb gives in, spilling all over Chris's hand and Scott's stomach.

"Told you it would work." Only Chris could smirk like that just before he comes. Caleb would hit him, but he can't fucking move. He's not even going to make it back to the bedroom. Through the haze, he can hear Chris pull out and toss away his condom.

"Y'all still have to shower," Chris says, soft and quiet and Caleb remembers the way he talked to Scott right after that first time he watched them fuck on the couch—only he doesn't feel like he shouldn't be hearing it this time.

"If you wanted me to shower, you shouldn't have done *that*," Scott mumbles into his neck and Chris chuckles.

"We already changed the sheets and you're both really gross now. You're showering. Come on, babe." Chris eases Scott off him, reaching around to press his hand on Caleb's hip to hold him steady. He waits until Caleb's settled on the counter leaning back against the mirror before he moves Scott to the shower. Caleb watches them through the steamed glass, following the path Chris's hands take over Scott's body as he washes away sweat and come and lets his eyes drift closed as Chris rinses shampoo out of Scott's hair.

"Hey, darlin'. Your turn," Chris says, one hand pressed against his cheek as he opens his eyes. He must have dozed off in the middle of Scott's shower. If he whines when Chris wraps both arms around him and pulls him to his feet, it's one hundred percent Chris's fault for making him move.

Chris holds him close in the shower, back pressed against Chris's chest as Chris rubs soap-slick hands over him.

"Turn around for me," Chris whispers, leading him around so Chris can wash his back. He winces just a little when Chris rubs over the bruise that's forming from his back being pressed against the frame of the mirror.

"I hurt you?"

"S'nothing."

"You can tell me or I can search out all the places you might be hurting until I figure it out."

"Just a little bruised where my back was hitting the mirror."

Chris pulls him closer and turns him a little to get a better look. His fingertips ghost over the bruise when he finds it.

"You're a little scraped up too. Why didn't you say anything?"

"I was kinda enjoying getting fucked. It's fine, really." Chris is really making him do a hell of a lot more talking than he'd like. He sighs and nuzzles his face into Chris's neck, hoping Chris will drop it.

"Wore you out more than I thought. You slept last night, didn't you?" Chris asks and Caleb nods into his neck. He can still smell *Chris* under the smell of soap. He missed that. "You been sleeping okay in New York?"

Caleb shrugs and feels Chris's lips trail over his forehead. Chris whispers something, but he's not really paying attention, and it's hard to care when he's got strong fingers massaging shampoo into his hair. It smells like his shampoo even though he doesn't remember bringing any over.

"Close your eyes," Chris says just before tilting his head back to wash the shampoo out, fingertips brushing over Caleb's face to wipe away the water when he's finished.

Chris leans him against the shower wall as he shuts off the water and towels them both dry.

"Tile's cold." Caleb frowns and Chris smiles, leaning forward to kiss him.

"Sorry. Come on; the bed's warmer."

Scott's already in bed watching TV when Chris walks him in the room. He expects Chris to push him in first, but when Scott pulls back the covers, Chris slides in first and pulls Caleb in after him.

"Thought you didn't sleep in the middle," Caleb mumbles but he lets Chris pull him close against his side anyway.

"I'm not sleeping. I think that's just you." Chris kisses the top of his head and rubs over his back, so he gives up and snuggles into Chris's chest.

"You just want us both. Greedy."

"Says the guy who always sleeps in the middle."

"I'm pretty sure you're the one who put me there."

"Easier than fightin' Scott for you. He's just too tired to fight right now."

"So full of shit," Scott mumbles, but he laughs from his own place on Chris's other side and reaches across Chris to rest his hand on Caleb's arm.

"Why is there talking anyway? Weren't y'all too tired to shower by yourselves just a few minutes ago?"

CHAPTER 13

CALEB wakes up to the soft twang of Chris's voice mixing with Scott's guitar. He doesn't recognize the song. Maybe it's something new they're working on, because they pause every few minutes to scratch something down on paper.

"Good nap?" Chris asks, trailing his hand over Caleb's back even though Caleb never opened his eyes.

"Yeah. Sorry." He doesn't remember falling asleep, but he'd expected Scott to pass out too.

"S'okay. Thought Scott was gonna join you, but five minutes of watching you sleep and he had to write a song about it."

"Chris wrote half the lyrics." Scott's sitting cross-legged on the bed with his guitar in his lap and he smiles when Caleb looks at him.

"Because I'm not singing it if it sounds like a bad romance novel," Chris says, but he leans over to make some changes in the songbook they're sharing. Scott tries the new notes and nods.

Caleb relaxes against Chris's side and doesn't answer. They don't usually write when he's around and until now it was something he'd given up being a part of, but Scott winks at him when Chris adds more to the song. Scott starts to play again, maybe from the beginning, and Chris doesn't join in when he first starts to sing. Scott rolls his eyes and starts over and the next time Chris joins in, his voice harmonizing with Scott's as they move through the song.

They probably won't ever record this. They don't record half the stuff they write. Scott has stacks and stacks of notebooks and only a few songs he's ever satisfied with. Once Caleb found a notebook with the original draft of their biggest single before Scott changed it to make it look like he wrote it about a girl. And this one? He's not even sure they could change it and not lose the whole thing. Maybe he can talk them into recording a demo of it just for him to take back to New York.

"Jason called," Chris says after they finish the song. "He wants to know if we're coming to his show."

"Tomorrow?" Caleb asks because he *does* want to see his friends. He's just not sure he wants to see them yet.

"Yeah. He's having everyone over later. Bought a lot of beer," Chris answers, sliding down on the bed so he can lie down. His fingers travel over Caleb's back as he talks.

"Sounds good."

"I gotta do some headshots for one of Danielle's friends tomorrow, and meet with someone at the club to work out some things for our next show, but I'll be back around five." Chris leans down for a kiss, his lips just brushing over Caleb's. He's not going to be disappointed. If Chris really took the whole five days off, they'd probably be ready to kill each other before he left.

"I should go to my place anyway and figure out what else I want to take to New York."

"Want help?" Scott looks back as he puts away his guitar, like he thinks Caleb might actually say no after spending a week alone in his hotel room.

"Yeah, sure. Someone has to make sure I pack clothes that match." Not that he's ever given a shit. He's not the one in front of the camera, but everyone else seems to care. Scott laughs and climbs back on the bed, stretching out on Chris's other side. Chris rolls his eyes when Scott snuggles against him and reaches over to run his hand over Caleb's jaw, but Caleb can see him fighting a smile anyway.

❧❧❧

DANIELLE jumps on him as soon as he walks into the bar and holds on tight.

"It's been a week. You're being stupid."

"Oh, you thought it was because I missed you? You're not that cool," Danielle says, pulling back and smirking. "I just couldn't take another day of Chris acting like an asshole and denying it was about you being gone."

"Funny. Like I even had time to see you last week," Chris says.

"You mean Jason and I avoided you after you spent a whole night bitching at everything." Danielle giggles as she turns to Caleb. "It was kind of cute at first when he was just all pouty. But then he started blaming inanimate objects for being in his way."

"She's exaggerating," Chris says, but there's not a lot of conviction in it as he shifts so his arm is brushing against Caleb's.

"She is, but not by much," Jason says as he and Scott walk up. "We're still glad you're back though."

"Fucker. We should have told the club we were here to see the opening act."

ℰᴑᴕ

THEY haven't gotten wasted at Jason's since all three of them started fucking. They've gotten buzzed, but Chris always stopped early to drive them home, which only made it more obvious that he was trying to keep Jason from asking Caleb about their relationship.

But it already happened and they survived it, so Caleb isn't too shocked when Chris says they'll just crash on the pull-out couch and go home in the morning before grabbing yet another beer.

It's not a real party, which is better anyway because Chris always keeps his distance when they're around people they don't know. Jason's girl has been around enough times to find out about them and Caleb's pretty sure Chris has some kind of blackmail information just in case she tries to sell them out. If he didn't, he wouldn't lean over to kiss Scott before sitting on Caleb's other side.

"You know what you're shooting when you get back?" Chris asks, letting his arm drape across the back of the couch behind Caleb so he can tangle his fingers in Scott's hair.

"Sort of… preparations for fashion week, the designers getting ready and all that. Then I'm shooting most of the shows for *Chic*."

"What are the chances they'll give you more time off?" Scott asks. Chris watches them, smiling, but Caleb can see him running his fingers through Scott's hair as Caleb turns his head to look at him.

"Pretty low, but then the next fashion week is in LA so I'll be around for all of that." Caleb can't help leaning over to kiss him. "I'll try for some more jobs in LA after that, but the best jobs are in New York."

"I know," Scott says, leaning in for another kiss and drawing it out.

"This is weird. I keep waiting for Chris to beat him up," Jason says from somewhere across from them. "I thought they might have a no kissing rule or something."

"Caleb's not a hooker, and come on, you think he'd put up with that?" Even Danielle wants to kill their mood.

"Not really. But it's still weird to see."

"Then stop watching," Caleb groans as he pulls back and lets his forehead fall on Scott's chest so he doesn't have to look at them. "We can hear you, you know."

"Chris didn't. He was too busy watching. Like he actually wanted you to make out with Scott. Crazy shit."

"Is it less weird if I kick your asses for watching them?" Chris growls.

"You're in my living room. What do you want me to do?"

"Go make out with your girlfriend before I start thinking you'd rather be with my boys."

ಬಿ

IT'S cold when Caleb wakes up. There's just one blanket thrown over them, so he moves closer to Scott and drapes over his chest. His back is only cold for a second before Chris follows, lying over Caleb's back.

Scott must be waking up too because his arm comes up to wrap around Caleb and his lips press against Caleb's forehead. But he sighs and lets his head rest against Caleb's, so he must not be against Caleb's plan of falling back asleep.

Scott's already drifted off again and Caleb's just about to follow when Jason's voice interrupts.

110

"I can't believe we all lost. Maybe they don't always sleep like this. Maybe they just fell this way because they were wasted."

"No way. They're all snuggly and comfortable. We just underestimated Chris's ability to share." And Danielle's, of course.

"Maybe they don't always sleep the same way. They have Caleb in the middle now because he's been gone," Jason says.

"You just don't want to be wrong. It makes sense, you know? Chris and Scott already had sides of the bed, so they put Caleb in the middle. Plus, you need to get over thinking they aren't going to stick with Caleb. They're all obviously totally in love with each other. Maybe Chris and Scott like that they can share Caleb if he's in the middle. It's sweet." Only Danielle would call them *sweet*.

"You think?"

"Well, Chris and Scott are in love with him at least. It's hard to tell with Caleb," Danielle answers. He sure as hell isn't letting them know he's awake now. Danielle will probably actually ask him if he's in love, and he's not sure what he'd answer. "Come on. I'm hungry. And if Chris wakes up and finds us staring at them, he's probably going to have a fit."

At least Chris is sleeping pretty hard against him because he really doesn't want to know what Chris would say about that. Caleb sighs and wills his body to relax again. It's not like he can get up and face them all now anyway.

CHAPTER 14

"SO WERE you good or do I have even more to cover up now?" Jessie asks as soon as he walks into her apartment on his first day back.

"Funny."

"It's a fair question." Jessie smirks and even pulls his T-shirt aside to check.

"I was good."

"Yeah, right. But at least you didn't get any new hickeys," Jessie says as she starts taking out fruit for breakfast. "So, did you have fun with your mystery person?"

"It was nice to be home."

"You're gonna be like that, huh?" Jessie smirks.

Caleb shrugs, and Jessie just rolls her eyes as she stabs a piece of cantaloupe with her fork. "So I was talking to Alicia yesterday. She was doing makeup for the spread about skinny jeans on guys, which I still say makes them look like flamingos."

"Is there a point to this?" With Jessie, there's always a chance he can tune her out for a good ten minutes before she notices.

"Yes! The point is that she said there was this hot new guy shooting it. I guess they gave up on the idea that you'd move back to New York and just hired a new staff photographer. He's supposed to be working with you all the way until fashion week. They're hoping you can pass on your amazing eye before you run off to LA again. Though Caitlyn says they'd still hire you back if you wanted. They could just push Vince back to *TeenChic* or something. They've been hoping you'd come back since, well, you know."

Jessie falls silent for the first time all morning. She might as well have just come out and said that everyone expected him to run back to New York after the actor he chased to LA dumped him. It wasn't like he hadn't thought about it. He'd been damn close to doing just that when Jason had found him. Then he'd met Scott and forgotten about all the reasons living in LA didn't make sense.

"Caleb." Jessie pokes his elbow with her fork. "You aren't allowed to mope about Damian when you have some other guy waiting for you in LA. Hell, they probably hired this guy because you spent the whole week you were here texting your boyfriend."

"You think everyone knows?"

"Okay, fine. They don't *know*, but everyone kind of suspects you aren't staying in LA just to prove a point anymore."

℘Ↄ

WHEN he checks in at the office, Caleb's glad Jessie warned him about his new shadow. Vince is already there and the second Wilkes introduces them, he knows Chris is going to be mad. Vince is tall with shaggy brown hair and Caleb can hear his Texas accent. It's not as pronounced as Chris's, but it's stronger than his own, and even though Caleb isn't interested, he can't pretend Vince isn't something to look at. Add in that he's got about an inch of height on Chris and a little more muscle, and Caleb figures that he'll be walking around with hickeys again if he can't figure out a way to make Chris not freak out.

It doesn't help that Vince spends the next two weeks trying to get him to hang out after shoots, and he can't tell if Vince is trying to hit on him or if he just doesn't have any friends in New York.

"Dude, come on. You can't just sit alone in your hotel all night. I heard your friend Jessie say she has a date tonight." Vince only knows that because Jessie made Caleb invite him to go to lunch with them after he stood next to Caleb like a lonely puppy.

Still, Caleb decides that until he can find out a way to figure out if Vince is straight, it's better if he just keeps turning Vince down when he asks him to hang out. Jessie's going to call him an anti-social asshole, but that's better than what Chris will say.

Besides, maybe he likes being able to call Chris and Scott at night. If anyone ever asks, he plans to tell them it's just for the phone sex. Chris will back up his story even if he's the one who calls Caleb when he runs late. When the phone rings, Caleb leaves Vince and sneaks behind a rack of coats. Vince doesn't really need someone looking over his shoulder the whole time anyway.

"So your flight comes in on Friday?" Chris asks, even though Caleb's told him and e-mailed Scott the flight number a week ago. His schedule has been annoying since he came back. They're paying for his hotel again, so Wilkes figures she can call him whenever she wants. If he's not shooting something somewhere, then she wants him to tag along with Vince. Even though Caleb's just contracted for the next two months and Vince is actually hired on *Chic's* staff, Vince is new and Wilkes doesn't trust him yet. Next time, he's just going to turn down the hotel and crash with Jessie. So it's been two weeks, and he was about to just fly for a day and give up sleep when they finally promised him a long weekend off.

"Yeah. I have a shoot in the morning on Friday and then I'll go to the airport from here."

"Good. Scott's got a show Saturday, but that's the only time I'm letting you out of bed."

"Sounds good," Caleb laughs. If it was anything but one of Scott's shows, he'd say they weren't leaving Scott's place at all.

"Hey! Caleb!" Vince comes around the corner grabbing Caleb's arm and pulling as he passes by. "One more shoot and then we're free. You coming out tonight?"

Caleb shakes his head and points to the phone, but Vince ignores him.

"Dude. You never come out! How are you ever going to get a girl at this rate? Come on. I know where we can find you a girl."

"Caleb." Chris might as well just growl and reach through the phone to punch Vince in the face.

"Hold on a sec," Caleb says, tilting the phone away from his lips and pulling away from Vince.

"You putting me on hold so you can make plans?" Chris says, but Caleb ignores him anyway.

"Vince. Give me a second to finish this. I'll be right back. I promise. Set up without me. You're doing fine anyway," Caleb says, and Vince shrugs, letting him go and nodding before walking away.

"Thinking about picking up some girls?" Chris asks.

"No. Maybe Vince is, but I'm too wiped to go out anyway."

"So you're going home just because you're tired?" Chris can really be a fucking idiot.

"This time? No. I'm going home because I'd rather talk to you and Scott. But even if I did go out, it shouldn't be a big deal because you should know I'm not going to be picking up girls."

"You been going out with him?"

"I'm about to because you're being a bastard, but no. I haven't felt like going out with him, but fuck, if I want to, I will. Just to

115

hang out. Not to pick anyone up." Caleb sighs. "You should know better than that."

"I should know, huh?" Chris growls.

"Yes. Are we really gonna have this fight? Because it's fucking stupid." Caleb takes a deep breath. They've been like this for days. Scott's threatened more than once to not let them talk to each other without his supervision.

But Chris changes his tone. "Fuck. I'm sorry, darlin'. It's just been a long time. I know you can go out and not pick anyone up."

"Good. Because Scott might kill us if we fight with only three days left. But Friday. I'll be back on Friday and I'll call after I finish this shoot and go home."

℘℘℘

"I HATE my job," Caleb says when he calls Friday morning. He doesn't even give Chris a chance to say hello. He tried Scott first, but it went straight to voicemail.

"What? Shit. Tell me you're getting ready to go to the airport."

"It's raining and this is supposed to be a spring shoot. If it doesn't stop, we gotta come back and shoot tomorrow."

"I hate your job," Chris says just as Caleb hears a door slam in the background. Caleb hears them kiss and there's a click as Scott picks up an extension.

"I'm just going by the look on Chris's face, but I'm guessing you're not going to be on that plane," Scott says.

"I'll try to get a later flight, but I don't even know when I'm getting out of here. Hell, if we don't finish, I gotta be back tomorrow anyway."

116

"Shit." Scott sighs and Caleb can imagine his hand rubbing over his face.

"I'm sorry." It might not be his fault, but it's his stupid job keeping them apart. He should just tell them to fuck without him. They've gotta be sick of living how they are.

"No, it's not your fault. When do you get off again if you've gotta work tomorrow?"

"I'd end up with two days off, then working four more. I should have three off after that, and I'm coming home for those no matter what they say."

"Okay, we'll still hope that you can make a late flight. It'll be fine, darlin'," Chris says it, but there's a sigh after it.

Caleb's still trying to come up with a decent answer when Jessie ducks into the trailer, and plops down in the chair next to him. She smiles but leaves him alone and starts to sort though her makeup. At least he's not cornered on this job with just Vince. Chris freaks out less when he knows Jessie's working the same shoot.

"Yeah. I'll get back as soon as I can," Caleb answers.

"Someone just walk in?" Scott would be the one to notice something little like a change in his tone.

"Yeah. Jessie."

Jessie looks up when he says her name and mouths *sorry*. She points to the door in an offer to leave, but he shakes his head. Technically, he's the one invading her space.

"We'll let you get back to work. Call us when you know something?" Chris has to know there isn't much hope that he'll get home today. But he still tries to have some hope as they say goodbye and hang up.

"Sorry. Did I interrupt something?"

"It's your trailer." Caleb shrugs, pushing his phone back in his pocket.

"And I don't mind you hiding in it," Jessie says, but she's quiet as she organizes all her different pots and tubes. She's not quiet much.

"So is there some other reason you're not talking my ear off?" Jessie being silent just doesn't sit well with him at all.

"I can mind my own business."

"Since when?"

"Since I'm not sure I want to know what's going on with you." Jessie shrugs, still not looking at him.

"Why?"

"I'm trying to mind my own business here," she says, sitting back and crossing her arms over her chest. He can't help laughing.

"It's weird. You always ask questions."

"Which you never answer." Jessie cocks her head to the side when she looks at him. "Suddenly you want to answer?"

"I don't know what the question is." Why was he even pressing? It had to be about his relationship.

"It's just... when you first came back here, I asked you if I was helping you cheat on anyone, and I know it doesn't matter, because I would have covered the hickeys up for you anyway."

"You think I'm cheating?"

Jessie turns back to face the counter before she starts talking.

"Look, I've never tried to see anything. Really. It's just, sometimes when you get texts, I pick up your phone, and you get that smiley happy look, you know? And sometimes I see the name on the screen. I don't mean to, but you know, you don't get *that look* when Jason or Danielle texts you. But you get it for Scott *and* Chris. And yes, I notice that when you're on the phone you make sure you never say a name, but you have different tones. It's like you're dating two different people. I've been doing this job long enough to see a few people doing this kind of thing." Jessie sighs, getting up and sitting on the counter, facing him for the first time after her long ramble.

"You think I'm cheating." He'd be mad, but hell, she's not wrong about him seeing two people.

"You're not? Because if you aren't, you've at least got a crush on the side."

"It's," Caleb hesitates. No one outside their circle knows about them and he hasn't talked to Chris and Scott about telling her. Sure, they know he's friends with Jessie since he moved to New York years ago, but they don't actually know her like he does. "It's more complicated than that."

"Complicated how?"

"The whole thing where you don't tell a single person about this is really important. I will deny it."

"Duh. Did you forget all five years of our friendship that happened before you picked up and moved to LA?" Jessie rolls her eyes and nods for him to continue.

"I am dating both of them. Chris and Scott. But, it's not cheating."

"You're dating them both, but they know about each other?"

"Yeah, but, it's not just that. They're together too. We're all together."

"Huh. Like, all three of you? Together?" Jessie's eyes are a little wide, but she doesn't look disgusted.

"Yeah."

"So now you *really* have to tell me the whole story."

119

✣

"I CAN try to fly down for the last day and a half," Caleb says when he calls Scott on his way home. He was expecting to get them both, but Scott says Chris is out and doesn't offer anything else.

"No. By the time you get here, it'll just be one day and you'll just be exhausted. You can make it a few more days and come next week. I'll be okay."

"Okay." Caleb doesn't say that *he* won't be okay. He's the one by himself all the time.

"Jessie's okay, so at least someone up there knows what's going on. You're not alone up there, baby." Maybe, just maybe, Scott's not all okay with it either. At least there wasn't any panic when he sent Scott a text that Jessie knew.

"Yeah." The taxi pulls up to the hotel and Caleb hands the driver a roll of bills as he gets out. He should hang up and sleep, but he can't help hoping Chris will come home so he can at least say goodnight.

"You almost home?"

"Getting in the elevator."

"Yeah? I sent something to your room." Scott's done it more than once, but he's still always surprised. Even if it's usually just food because Scott thinks he doesn't eat enough when he's in New York.

"You didn't have to."

"I wanted to."

"And you want me to stay on the phone so you can hear my reaction when I see it?" Caleb already knows the answer. Scott's a sap like that.

"I'm in LA. I deserve it."

Caleb opens the door and looks around. He's expecting something on the table, but there's nothing. "Is it big? I'm not seeing anything, babe."

"It's… pretty damn noticeable. Look in the bedroom?"

"They put stuff in the bedroom?" Caleb asks, but he gasps as his eyes scan over the bed. "Scott."

Chris is stretched out on his stomach on the bed. He's asleep and he doesn't stir when Caleb runs a hand over his bare back.

"I realize he might be kind of annoying on his own, but I still have that show tomorrow." Scott laughs. "Is he already passed out?"

"Yeah. He'll miss your show."

"He's seen me play a million times and he's missed plenty of shows. You needed him more. You're alone too much. I'd have come with him if I could. He's there four days and then he's gotta come back for a show, but you'll be back a few days after that anyway. And then? *I* get to fuck you first."

"Fair enough." Caleb laughs and he wishes Scott was with them too, but he's not going to sleep alone and that's something. "Thanks."

"Of course. We know we need to come there some for you too. We should've tried to come see you before. It's not really fair to just leave all the work to you."

"Thanks." He still can't believe Chris is *here*, with him.

"You should get some sleep. Don't let him smother you to death once he wakes up enough to figure out you're there."

Caleb flips his phone closed and pushes off his jeans. Chris doesn't wake when he climbs under the covers. He's a damn heavy sleeper and it's not until Caleb combs through his hair that Chris's eyes blink open.

"Hey," Chris sighs and leans into his hand.

"Hey." Caleb leans in for a slow, sleepy kiss.

"Time?"

"One a.m." So much for an early day. "I got stuck going over proofs at the studio. I would've left if I knew you were here. I was trying to get some work done in case I could get a flight tomorrow."

"S'late. Come here," Chris mumbles and pulls at Caleb until he can spoon against Caleb's back. "Tomorrow, we'll call Scott and see how much he'll let us do. Got a feeling he wants to pay you back for how much you like to make us tease."

Chapter 15

WHEN Caleb's alarm goes off, he rolls over to turn it off and smiles when he has to climb over Chris. Chris groans, wrapping an arm around him and holding him close.

"You gotta go into work?"

"Just for one shoot. We ran out of daylight yesterday."

Chris nods and rubs over his back a few times. "You gonna let me go with you or leave me here?"

"You can come. Everyone knows we're friends. As long as you manage to keep your hands to yourself." It's not that he's ashamed of Chris; it's just that it won't seem right to have everyone thinking that Chris is his boyfriend and Scott's just his friend.

"Gonna have to unless we can get a hold of Scott. He says I'm not allowed to do more than kiss you until he says so. Bastard." Chris presses his lips to Caleb's forehead and Caleb can't help tilting his head up for a kiss. It's so fucking hard to not grind against him and ask for more. Fuck, he'd thought about how hard it had to be for them, but he didn't really get it before. It must drive them insane to wait for him after years of just being together.

"S'okay. It's not like we don't get anything. Not sure if Scott will be as generous as you over the phone though." Chris kisses him again before he sighs and lies back down. "We gotta get up now?"

123

"Yeah. If I don't want to listen to them bitch about me holding up the shoot."

"They should worry about listening to me bitch about them holding up you," Chris says as he pulls away and starts to get up.

"I think that might ruin our story about just being good friends."

❧❧

NO ONE says much about Chris being around. He knows enough about photography that he doesn't get in the way, and they're happy enough to have him around helping Caleb out since Vince is gone for the day. Apparently they'd already booked him for somewhere else, leaving him safe from Chris for another day. It isn't until he follows Caleb into the makeup trailer and notices only Jessie's inside that Chris closes the distance between them.

"You're in a better mood this morning," Jessie says, grinning as she cleans up her station and offers Caleb a seat.

"Yeah, um, this is Chris." Caleb nods to where Chris is leaning against the makeup counter in front of him.

"We've met." Chris smirks and exchanges a look with Jessie.

"What?"

"Who do you think helped me get into your room last night? It sure was convenient that you told her yesterday."

"You didn't tell me?" He turns on Jessie and she blushes.

"He said he wanted to surprise you. I couldn't ruin it. He made me promise! I swear it made sense at the time." Jessie frowns. "And you were happy right?"

"Yeah. I was happy." Caleb can't help smiling, but he still has to swat at Chris for his smug look.

"Good. And as a bonus, you look like you've actually slept. I'd thank him for that because you look awful with those dark circles, but I'm afraid I'm going to be coming over in the morning again so people don't think you're a whore who's dating a vacuum cleaner. Or were those his fault? I guess they could have been the other guy's fault."

"Oh, they were his fault all right." Caleb rolls his eyes toward Chris.

"Hey! Scott helped. At least one was his fault." Chris deserves to have Jessie glaring at him. "And I didn't make more work for you. It was too late when he finally got back."

"Fair enough. He's only got two days off. If you're doing it again, I expect you to do it when he's got time to heal a little. Wait until his four day break at least. Those things used up half my makeup." Jessie giggles and Caleb figures he's lucky she hasn't met Scott yet.

"Four days? My next break is three."

"Nope. They had an issue with one of the locations, so they moved some stuff around. You're shooting longer today though."

"Yeah?" Sure, it will mean longer before he can go back to the hotel with Chris and call Scott, but it will also mean one more day with all of them together later. "Does that mean you have to work late too?"

"Yep. I think there's a conspiracy against me ever going on a date. Not that my dates are interesting. I'm giving Drake two more weeks to make a move, and then one of you has to come help me figure out if he's gay."

"And how are we supposed to figure that out?" Chris reaches over to brush his fingers over Caleb's and frowns.

"I don't know. You've gotta have gaydar if you got Caleb. He's not so much closeted as he is just completely clueless when people hit on him." Jessie giggles.

"I believe that." Chris moved before Caleb could pinch him. "What? It's true, which is probably good for you actually, because I might have killed you if you actually responded to how much Scott used to flirt with you."

"Scott didn't flirt with me. If that was true, you would have killed me even if I ignored him."

"He did. Why do you think Jason stuck to you so much when I got back into town? He thought you were going to get your ass kicked once I found out you'd been hanging out with Scott the whole three weeks I was gone. Hell, Jason thought he was going to get his ass kicked for introducing you to Scott. He tried to convince me that you were straight for a while."

"Yeah? So why didn't you do anything?" Caleb asks because now that he thinks about it, he can remember how weird Jason was about him hanging out with Chris in the beginning.

Chris shrugs, not looking at Caleb when he answers. "Didn't hate you as much as I expected."

"So when do I get to meet Scott?" Jessie says when Caleb can't figure out any way to answer Chris. "Because it feels weird to only see you with Chris now. I feel like I'm missing something."

"I don't know. Are you going to plot with him behind my back too?"

"Obviously."

෨෬

EVEN though staying late means an extra day with Chris and Scott, Caleb still thinks the shoot takes way too long. By the time they get back to the hotel, he's already exchanged ten texts with Scott to make sure he'll answer right away. If they're too late, they'll have to wait until after Scott's show to call him and it's been way too long since Caleb got off from anything besides his own hand.

126

Chris grabs him as soon as they get back to his hotel room, pushing him against the wall and kissing him hard as he dials Scott.

"Tell me you boys didn't go and start without me," Scott says over the line, and Chris breaks away to put the phone on speaker.

"Just kissing. Kissing's allowed," Chris says between kisses down his neck.

"Hum. So you have gotten each other so worked up that you can't slow down?"

"Nope. We're good," Chris lies.

"And that's why the only thing I can hear from Caleb is him trying, and failing, to breathe normal."

"That's just how he sounds when I'm around. You've just forgotten because it's been a while."

"Yeah. Sure," Scott laughs. "Caleb, baby? How're you doing?"

"Good. We didn't start without you. We're just a little worked up. You know Chris. He fucking talked dirty all the way home." Chris hasn't stopped his assault on Caleb's neck and fuck, Scott needs to go ahead and catch up so they can get some clothes off.

"Hum. So you think I'm not going to make you wait at all after how much you like to tease us?" Scott's just evil.

"Mostly, I have you torture Chris," Caleb moans.

"Yeah. So what's he doing to you now?"

"Trying to give me a fucking hickey even though he promised not to." He should really push Chris off, but it's just been way too long for him to make himself care.

"Hum… you want me to tell him he has to stop? I say stop and you guys have to stop."

"Evil fucker," Chris growls. He's one to talk. He knows Scott's gonna tease them and he's working Caleb up anyway.

"Please," Caleb moans out. He's not letting Chris fuck this up for him. It's bad enough that he knows Scott is going to draw it out without Chris making him tease even more.

"You missed us, baby?" Scott asks like he doesn't already know.

"Yes, so fucking much. Miss you. Wish you could have come too." He'll say just about anything to get Scott saying what he wants.

"Me too, baby. Me too. Should I let Chris get you naked?"

"Yes. Yes, please." He's already pushing against Chris and they're never going to let him live it down if he comes from humping Chris's leg.

"Sounds like you're starting to lose it already. Chris? How're you doing?"

"It'd be really nice if you'd let me get him naked before he goes insane. You should see him. He can't even stay still he wants it so bad. I think he's been missing us." Chris's breath is a little short but the fucker is in more control than Caleb likes. Caleb makes a note to make sure they both have to wait forever the next time he's calling the shots.

"I hate you both," Caleb moans into the kiss Chris gives him.

"No you don't," Scott chuckles, and Caleb would really think about hating him if his next words weren't, "All right. Get him naked on the bed. Caleb, you can get Chris naked too. I know you want to."

That's all they need. Chris throws the phone on the bed and they start pulling on each other's clothes. Fuck. He's missed Chris's hands all over him, gentle as they graze over his side even as he's pushed roughly onto the bed. Chris pulls back, kneeling above him and waiting.

"You gonna tell me what I get to do?" Chris asks.

"No touching his dick. Not until I say so. But you can kiss everywhere else." Scott says. Caleb can hear his breath catch. Good, if he can get Scott worked up, Scott will give him what he wants. Caleb moans as Chris starts to kiss down his chest and settles for sucking on his hip.

"Scott? You naked yet? Wanna think about you." Caleb's lucky his phone works well on speaker because he doesn't have the energy to find where they dropped it.

"Yeah, baby. Can't help touching myself when you sound like that. Wish I could be there."

"Wish you were here too. Just a few days and you're gonna fuck me so good. Can't wait to have you again."

"Fuck yeah. Tell me what he's doing to you."

"Licking all around my dick. Fuck… and my balls. Takes you damn literally." Caleb moans as Chris licks lower.

"You thought I was making it up when you were in charge?" Scott lets out a low chuckle, followed by a moan.

"You've been getting it a hell of a lot more often," Caleb bites out as Chris moves back up, sucking and licking over the crease of his leg. "Come on. Please."

Begging has always worked with Scott eventually and Caleb's not surprised when Scott moans and says, "Yeah, yeah. Chris, suck him off. You know what he wants."

Chris doesn't hesitate in swallowing him down, his hands pushing hard on Caleb's hips to hold him down when Caleb can't help bucking up. Chris's mouth is so wet and hot and ten fucking times better than his own hand.

Caleb knows he's moaning, but it's not long before Scott's just as loud over the phone. Chris has already caved and started jacking himself off when Caleb chokes out a warning and comes hard in his mouth. Chris swallows and kisses back up to his neck to where the phone has rolled next to Caleb's ear.

129

"You get off with him or you still going, babe?" Chris asks. He can barely even hear through the haze he's still coming back from.

"Almost there," Scott groans. "You?"

"Same. You got a preference on how I finish?"

"On him. His chest, his stomach. Just come on him," Scott gasps.

"Fuck yeah." Chris sits up just enough to jack himself over Caleb's chest until he finally grunts and spills over him. "Looks so good with my come all over him, babe. I'd take pictures for you if he'd let me."

"Fuck!" Scott's breath catches, and they're silent for a minute before Caleb speaks.

"Chris better be planning to get up and clean this off me. Because it's going to stop being hot and start being gross soon."

Chris laughs. "Yeah, yeah. I got it."

"You know, I still have to go out and play tonight, fuckers," Scott says.

"Really not sorry," Caleb mumbles.

"Didn't expect you were. I'm gonna try to get an hour of sleep before I gotta get up again," Scott says when Chris comes back with a towel to clean him off.

"Yeah. Naps are good." Caleb sighs as Chris wraps around him and kisses his neck.

"Sounds like a plan," Chris agrees. "Call after the show if you want round two?"

ᔑᑐᗡ

CALEB wakes up with Chris pressed against his back, one arm wrapped tight around him. His breath tickles the hair on the back of

Caleb's neck. He's expecting to smell breakfast from the kitchen until he wakes up enough to remember that they're in New York and Scott's in LA.

So it's not everything, but having just Chris is a hell of a lot better than nothing. Hell, he actually feels like he slept a full night instead of waking up sore and freezing. Chris sighs and pulls him closer as he wakes up.

"Mornin'," Chris says, kissing Caleb's back before he lets go and turns on his back.

"Hey," Caleb mumbles as he turns around to face Chris. He isn't *trying* to cuddle. Later, he's going to tell Scott how Chris grabbed him and made him lay over Chris's chest.

"Sleep well?"

"Yeah." Though he hadn't been expecting to sleep through the night the first time. "Scott didn't call."

"He did. But he was half drunk and you were really passed out."

"You should've woken me up." He's not pouting. It's just that he doesn't want Scott to think he doesn't care. He knows what it's like to be the one who's alone.

"I tried, darlin'. I promise." Chris chuckles and squeezes the arm around his back. "S'okay. We'll call him later."

Caleb shrugs. "What do you wanna do? Go out? See New York?" It's not that he hasn't spent a lot of time with Chris. But it's always in LA, where it's not like Chris expects to be entertained. And hell, most of the time, Scott's there.

"No. New York's boring. I want to stay in bed and order room service."

"You want to stay in bed and order room service?" He'd buy it more if they didn't have to wait for Scott to call to do anything resembling sex.

"Maybe watch some TV."

"Dude. I don't need a vacation. I've just had some busy days. I know what you're doing, and I don't need you to take care of me. If I looked tired when you got here, it was just because I had one day of hell."

"I didn't say that. Maybe *I'm tired*. Jet lag and all that. I need to recover."

"Uh huh."

"I'm the guest, so I get to pick what we do. And you can't argue, because Scott says if we fight while he's not around to tell us we're being stupid, then he's killing us both."

"Fine. We stay in bed and order room service." Caleb rolls his eyes, but he doesn't resist when Chris turns on his side and pulls him up for a kiss. He licks along Caleb's lips until Caleb lets him in, but Chris doesn't deepen the kiss like Caleb is used to. Instead, he lets his tongue slip in and out of Caleb's mouth, kissing with his lips more than his tongue as his thumb brushes over Caleb's cheek. Caleb laughs as he pulls away. "Since when do you kiss like a girl?"

"Since Scott's not home and we can't get worked up. Can't call him for a couple more hours." Chris sighs, kisses him again, and this time Caleb lets it stretch out longer.

"This is how you make it when I have to work a lot." It probably makes him an ass that he's never thought about how they manage when some days he doesn't have the energy to do more than call and say goodnight.

"S'not that bad." Chris rolls his eyes and kisses him again. "Scott likes it."

CHAPTER 16

SCOTT makes Chris drive when they pick him up from the airport a week later.

"You know, last time, you made me wait until we got home," Chris says when Scott pulls Caleb in the back seat after him.

"Last time, neither of us had seen him. You saw him two days ago. I haven't seen him in almost a fucking month." Scott kisses him as soon as the door closes, hot and desperate as he runs his hands over Caleb's face and down his chest.

"You still can't fuck in the backseat while I drive. I'll crash," Chris says, but he leans back to run a hand through Scott's hair as they kiss.

"I'll be good," Scott answers, staying close enough that his lips brush Caleb's as he talks.

"Yeah. Sure. Shirts stay on or I'm pulling over."

By the time they get home, Scott's already argued with Chris four times about what exactly it means for Caleb's shirt to be on. According to Scott, it just means that it's touching some part of his body. Either way, Caleb pulls it back down when they get home, because he's not walking into Scott's place half dressed. He doesn't need to attract that much attention from the neighbors.

133

They've all been hard for a while by the time they get inside, and Chris pushes between Scott and him as soon as the door closes behind them.

"Y'all are trying to kill me," he moans as he kisses Scott and then Caleb before pushing them both toward the bedroom. They fight with clothes as they walk, leaving a trail down the hallway and ending up naked by the time they get to the bed.

"Missed you." Scott pushes him onto his back, leaning down to kiss him hard. Chris falls down next to them so he can push into the kiss, and it's so great to have them both again. It's hot and sweaty and so much better than his cold hotel room in New York.

"Scott made me promise he got to fuck you first." Chris smirks and reaches to where the lube is already out on the bedside table. "But I'm sure as hell gonna help."

Chris's finger is cool as it presses into him, but he still pushes back. It's been too long since he's gotten fucked and none of them are in the mood to go any slower than they have to.

With Scott, he's used to everything being drawn out, but this time Scott fucks him hard and fast, no teasing and waiting until he's begging. He comes over Chris's hand too fast, but neither of them can talk because Scott comes right after him, and it only takes a few minutes with both of their mouths fighting over Chris's cock before his come ends up on both of their faces.

"If there's come in my hair, I'm kicking your ass," Scott says, but he's laughing as he and Caleb crawl back up the bed.

"You're the ones who put your heads there. If you didn't want my come on you, you should've made sure it ended up in someone's mouth."

"Maybe we thought you'd take longer," Scott teases, getting up to wash off his face.

"Says the guy who'd already gotten off. Besides, it's not really my fault you got so much. Caleb didn't get so much on him. You must've wanted it." Chris laughs and wipes off Caleb's cheek, moaning when Caleb sucks the come off his fingers. Scott shakes his head and chuckles, not bothering to argue.

"I get to pick how we do it next," Caleb says, sighing against Chris.

"Fair enough." Chris kisses him before nudging him onto his side and wrapping around him. One day, he's going to point out how much Chris likes to spoon—except then Chris will probably point out that Caleb never objects all that much to being the little spoon.

"I'm just looking forward to being able to breathe while I sleep," Scott says as he climbs back into bed on Caleb's other side and shifts until his head's tucked just under Caleb's chin. "It's like he doesn't remember you're thinner than me when we sleep. He tries to hold me as tight when you're not here."

ℰℛ

CALEB doesn't argue when Chris settles on the bed after breakfast and flips on the TV, but Scott objects when Chris flips it to ESPN Classic.

"*This* is what we're watching? Why do you need to watch old games? You already know what happens."

"That's not the point." Chris rolls his eyes and tosses the remote out of reach.

Scott starts to complain again, but Caleb's really not in the mood to listen to them bicker about something stupid. He's too sleepy and comfortable to find out if they'll laugh it off or let it escalate to something that leads to them snapping at each other for a couple hours, so he pulls Scott's head onto his chest so he can run his fingers through Scott's hair.

"Cheater," Scott mumbles, but he sighs as Caleb pulls out the elastic he'd tied his hair back with and combs through the hair at the base of his neck.

"You don't want to fight anyway." Caleb chuckles a little when Scott lets out a soft moan.

"Maybe I did. Maybe he gets his way too often."

"Sorry. You want me to stop playing with your hair so you can fight?" Caleb offers and Chris laughs at the idea before leaning over to kiss him.

"Shut up. It's still cheating," Scott says, swatting at Chris's leg before he lets his eyes close.

"Hasn't been easy without you here. I've been thinking we should try to make it up to New York more next time," Chris says after a few minutes.

"Yeah?" Caleb looks up from Scott's face to meet Chris's eyes.

"If it's okay with you, and we won't be in the way too much. We can write while you're working just as well in New York as we can here."

"Yeah. If you won't be bored when I'm working." Caleb feels himself smiling and when he looks down, Scott's smiling a little too.

"Good. Because we might not get as much time next month as we thought."

"You got something?" Caleb tries not to look disappointed. Hell, he has no right when it's his job that kept them apart for the last month.

"I got a few shows booked next month." Chris looks down at Scott before he adds, "in Europe."

"Dude, that's awesome." He might still be stuck in New York for half of that time anyway. "You just heard?"

136

"Day after I got back here. Just wanted to wait and tell you in person, darlin'." Chris pulls him into a kiss and smoothes a hand over his hair.

"How long?"

"I'll be out about three weeks. Scott was gonna tag along with me the first week, and then maybe hang out in New York with you the week he comes back."

"You guys are lucky I'm willing to follow your asses around," Scott mumbles, but he still leans into the hand Caleb's got in his hair.

"That's just because you like our asses." Chris laughs and rubs his hand in Scott's hair with Caleb's until Scott sighs and snuggles against Caleb's chest.

"Um hum. When you have old wrinkled asses, I'm just going to chill out in LA when you're gone."

"Oh, that's how it's gonna be?" Chris smirks and moves down so he's even with Scott on the bed.

"Yeah," Scott says just before Chris kisses him. Caleb can see his tongue slip into Scott's mouth as they kiss, dragging it out until Chris slides a hand up his leg to feel how hard they've made him.

"I think I remember you saying it was your call how we did it next," Chris says, looking up at him when he breaks away from Scott.

"Wanna watch you fuck him." In the beginning, Caleb thought he'd hate watching them together. He couldn't help thinking it was something he'd never be a part of, but in the end he loved knowing that he got to see them in a way no one else ever did. Never once has he gotten the idea that they are holding something back since he's been watching.

"I can sure as hell do that." Chris helps Scott climb over him as he lies down all the way on the bed. "You got a preference how?"

"Like this," Caleb says, pulling Scott on his side to face away from Chris. Before them, he'd never been much for spooning sex. He'd always felt weird if he couldn't see who he was fucking. Not that he'd tell Chris that. Chris would make fun, but really, it wasn't weird to want to see the person you were fucking. Chris was just weird.

But involving three people in sex kind of changed his opinion about spooning. It's the only position on the bed that lets them all get equal attention without doing some kind of crazy circus sex— not that Chris is ever going to stop trying.

"Been a while," Chris says as he pulls off the loose pajama pants Scott had thrown on to make breakfast.

"Sorry." If they haven't fucked since the last time he left, then they're going on almost four weeks.

"Not blamin' you, darlin'. Just saying." Chris passes him the lube, leaning over Scott for a long kiss.

Scott moans and reaches for his neck, breaking his kiss with Chris and taking Caleb's mouth for himself as Caleb strokes over the length of his cock. Chris reaches around, linking his hand with Caleb's and pulling until Scott is moaning into Caleb's mouth.

"Come on. Get him ready for me before he gets off without us," Chris chuckles, smoothing Scott's hair back from his face.

"Not that gone, asshole." Scott turns to glare at Chris, but he doesn't object when Chris kisses him.

Scott opens to his fingers easily, pushing into Chris's fist as he fucks himself on Caleb's fingers. "I'm good. Get on with it already."

"S'what happens when it's been a while." Chris smirks at Caleb as he rolls a condom over his cock and takes the lube from Caleb.

"Like you haven't been jacking off four times a day." Scott moans as Chris pushes into him, gripping Caleb's hip and throwing his head back against Chris's shoulder.

Caleb's sure he'll never get tired of watching them together. There's something about how they push and bite, but Chris never stops watching Scott to make sure it's good; to make sure he's got Scott shaking just as much as he wants.

"Fucks you just the same way," Scott whispers into his mouth, breaking off in a moan as Caleb strokes him. Scott reaches down to return the favor. It's almost true. Chris does the same over-protective shit, always watching him, checking that he's okay even though it's not like he's ever freaked out before. But it's still different with Scott. Chris is more confident with Scott. He's already worked out all of Scott's favorite places and knows just how to get him off when he wants it fast, or slow him down when he wants to drag it out.

But Caleb doesn't argue. Instead he pushes against Scott until he can hold both of their cocks together in his hand, jacking them hard and fast until Scott comes over his hand and his cock. Scott knocks his hand away as he comes down, spreading hot come over Caleb's cock and pulling until Caleb comes, warm and messy over his stomach and chest.

"So hot together," Chris moans and bites at Scott's neck, kissing and sucking as he thrusts harder.

"Fuck, I love you." It's low and muffled in Scott's hair, but Caleb still hears Chris say it. Scott's smile is small and he covers it with a sigh, but Caleb's sure he heard it also, and he doesn't look surprised.

Of course he doesn't. They've been together on an off for three years and they'd been going nine months solid when they let him in. Of course they've said it before. He knew this. He *assumed* it.

But they've never said it in front of him, probably because they've also never said it *to* him.

"Gonna shower," Caleb mumbles, pushing away and getting out of bed.

"Be there in a minute," Scott says behind him, but Caleb knows if he hurries, he can be out before Scott makes it out of bed.

He turns the water up and he knows his skin is going to turn red from the heat, but it's better than thinking about what he heard. It's better than thinking about why he even cares. Because he knew this. He knew they were in love with each other when he agreed to do this, and he knew they couldn't be in love with him right away. Hell, he wasn't in love with them then either.

Except that it's been two months and maybe now he is—in love—with two people who are in love with each other.

He's really screwed.

CHAPTER 17

CALEB makes it out of the shower just as Scott's opening the door, and he doesn't miss the disappointment on Scott's face.

"Sorry. Shower with Chris?" Caleb kisses the frown on Scott's face. Caleb needs some space, but he hates to see Scott look like that. Probably because he's in love with Scott.

"Yeah. Shower's too small for all three of us anyway. Next place, I promise we'll get a better shower." Scott smiles and kisses him again, so Caleb figures he's forgiven.

Chris raises an eyebrow when he steps back into the bedroom.

"That was quick."

"Yes. So I've heard. Get in the shower so he doesn't spend all his time thinking I'm an ass because I showered too fast."

Chris must buy it, because he just laughs and goes to shower, brushing against Caleb as he passes by.

Leaving while they're in the shower is an asshole thing to do. Caleb knows this. He really does. He likes to think that leaving them a note that says he's just got some business to take care of while he's in town makes it a little better, but he's pretty sure it's not going to help much.

141

Either way, he has to get some space, or they're going to figure out something is wrong. And he really can't have them *apologizing* for being in love with each other and not him. It's stupid, and it's not like he didn't know it from the beginning.

Scott calls before he even makes it to his apartment, but he lets it go to voicemail and doesn't listen. Later he'll tell Scott that he left his phone in the car.

Chris calls five minutes later, and Caleb can picture him hiding somewhere to call because he's sure Chris told Scott that everything was probably fine. Which is why he really doesn't listen to the voicemail Chris leaves him.

The problem is that there's nothing to do at his apartment. Scott came by after he went to New York and cleaned out his refrigerator, so all he has is a bottle of ketchup and four cans of coke.

He can't watch TV because he canceled his cable after he figured out that he was never going to spend more than twenty minutes in his apartment when he visited, and his guitar is at Scott's. He's trying to read a book and failing when Jason calls.

He shouldn't pick up, but Jason's his friend. Sure, Jason's friends with Chris and Scott, but he's always taken to Caleb since they met. If he's calling on behalf of Chris and Scott, Caleb can convince him to not report back.

"Hey. Damn. Didn't expect you to actually pick up the phone," Jason says when he picks up.

"Then why'd you call?"

"I was going to leave a voicemail and tell you I'm playing Sunday night. Though I figured I'd be lucky if Chris let you out of the house. He's been jumpy as hell. I think Scott sent him to you half because they were worried about you and half because Chris was driving him insane without you."

"Yeah? E-mail me the details. I'll show." Caleb hopes Jason will ignore that Caleb skips over the part about Chris and Scott.

"With Chris and Scott?"

"Don't know. Haven't asked them."

"You haven't asked them? Caleb, what's going on? They've spent the last month moping around and pretending they weren't sending you texts every five minutes. Where are they?"

"Probably at Scott's?"

"Okay. Where are *you*?" Jason asks.

"My apartment. I still have my own apartment, you know."

"Yeah. Scott goes by once a week to turn lights on and move your car so no one breaks in. And sometimes, they sleep in your bed instead of going home."

"They don't do that." If they did, they sure as hell wouldn't tell Jason.

"They do. I've picked Scott up from your apartment three times in the morning. And Chris's truck was parked outside, which I'm pretty sure means Chris was still asleep in your bed. Because when I take Scott back to his apartment, the truck's always back."

"Whatever."

"Caleb."

"I'm not a girl. I don't wanna talk, dude. Aren't you supposed to be the straight one with a girlfriend?"

"Okay. Whatever you say. But I'm expecting to see you at the show."

℘◌

CHRIS and Scott don't bother to knock. It could have something to do with how he's been gone four hours and he still hasn't called either of them back. He's staring at the pizza he ordered when he hears the door unlock. He should meet them at the door, but he freezes instead. By now they have to know something's wrong and he still doesn't have an answer for them.

When they find him in the living room, Chris leans against the door frame and watches while Scott sits next to him on the couch.

"We figured out why you left, but I really wish you'd have just said something," Scott says.

"Or answered your fucking phone. You can't answer for us, but you can answer for Jason?" Chris glares. Caleb's going to kill Jason when he sees him again.

"Chris. Not the point," Scott says, and Chris shuts up.

"You don't have to say anything," Caleb says before Scott can continue. "I just needed some space, but it's not like I didn't already know. I knew."

"Baby, you think we don't love you too? Shit. Caleb. Just because we haven't said it doesn't mean we haven't been thinking about it. I love you, okay?" When he doesn't answer, Scott puts a hand on Caleb's cheek and turns him so he can't look away. Later, he knows Scott's going to point out that they could have fixed this a lot easier, but fuck. He never even fucking considered that they'd thought about it too. *He* hadn't really thought about it before today. "We both do. Chris just doesn't say it much. Except that sometimes he slips and says it when we're having sex. Hell, I thought that was how you'd end up finding out. It's how he finally told me the first time."

"Thanks. Make me sound like an asshole," Chris interrupts.

"Look, you guys don't have to," Caleb starts, but Scott interrupts him.

"I love you. Stop arguing about it. I get enough shit from Chris." Scott rolls his eyes and Caleb can't help laughing. He spent four hours worrying for no fucking reason. Scott loves him, and even if Chris doesn't say it himself, it's something that he doesn't object to Scott saying it. Hell, it's not like he's not used to Scott speaking for Chris anyway.

"Okay, okay. I love you too." It's stupid and he doesn't want to think about if they sound like girls, so he just pulls Scott into a kiss instead of trying to look at him. But Scott still turns to look at Chris when he pulls away—even though he just told Caleb that Chris didn't say it. Caleb doesn't want Chris thinking he has to say it. "Dude. You really don't have to. It's fine."

Chris shakes his head, pushes off the door frame and walks toward them to sit on the coffee table in front of Caleb.

"Yeah. I kind of do have to say it this time. Because your stupid ass isn't going to believe it unless I do." Chris reaches out, cupping Caleb's cheek in his hand and looking right into his eyes. "I love you. I don't say it a lot, but I can say it when I need to. It's not like I've never said it to Scott when we aren't fucking. Just don't start thinking I'm going to say it every time we hang up the phone or something."

Caleb nods. Chris doesn't say shit like this, especially not staring right into his eyes, which is why he has to swallow before he can answer. "Yeah. It's fine. And... shit, I love you too."

Chris smirks when Caleb stumbles on his words and Caleb should hit him for that, but he's still too shocked to resist when Chris leans forward and kisses him long and slow.

"Now I damn well better get sex for this."

ℰℜ

"ARE y'all ever gonna stop making out so we can get up and go home? This bed isn't made for three people," Chris complains. Caleb considers telling Chris that he knows they sleep in his bed sometimes.

"You love it," Caleb says between kisses. If Chris really hated it, he'd have done something besides watch them kiss through their post-sex haze.

"We know you do." Scott laughs into Caleb's mouth, pulling away just enough to speak.

"I'm just here for the sex," Chris says, but he reaches over Caleb to tangle his fingers in Scott's hair as they kiss.

"Does he really think we buy that shit?" Scott presses his lips to Caleb's again, dragging it out a few seconds before Caleb can answer.

"Does he really think we buy *any* of his shit?"

"I should leave you both here and go sleep in Scott's bed by myself. A queen's fitting for y'all, but I need the king."

Chris deserves to have them laughing at him. Caleb should point out that he's the one who said "I love you" a second time when they were fucking. Chris just groans and turns away from them to lie on his back.

"You know that was the worst line ever, right?" Scott says through his laugh.

"I'm leaving you both here and locking you out of the house with the food."

"Naw, but we'll come with you. I want to eat in the morning." Caleb turns to lean over Chris and kiss him instead. For all his bitching, Chris doesn't hesitate in kissing back, bringing his hand up to hold Caleb to him. When Caleb pulls away, Chris tilts his head down to press his lips to Caleb's forehead.

"Come on, then. Let's get home."

ℰℴℭℛ

"I'M PISSED at you," Caleb says when they get to Jason's show on Sunday.

"You never specifically said that if they asked, I couldn't tell them where you were." Jason smirks and pulls him into a quick hug.

"It was implied."

"Sorry. I might feel bad if they weren't at the bar getting your drink for you. You guys are okay now?"

"Yeah. We're good." Caleb shrugs. At least Jason just nods and doesn't ask for details. "But you didn't have to butt in."

"Considering that you thought your apartment was a decent hiding place, combined with how they still hadn't figured out where you were, says otherwise."

CHAPTER 18

WHEN Chris texts him and says to call as soon as he's finished working, Caleb can't help worrying a little. It's usually Scott who does that, not Chris, so he texts Chris back while the model is changing to ask what's wrong.

Don't worry. Scott just can't keep his fucking mouth shut.

Chris is kind of an idiot at making sure he doesn't worry. So he texts Scott instead to ask if everything's okay.

Yeah. Just call later.

That's probably the shortest damn text Scott's ever sent, but at least he answered. If something was really wrong, Caleb likes to think he knows he could call and interrupt work if it was that big of a deal. Especially considering that Scott knows they just have him helping out Vince today. Vince doesn't even really need his help. The shoot he did the week Caleb was gone turned out amazing.

Caleb's thumb hovers above the call button on his phone, but he stops and snaps his phone closed instead. He's supposed to have an early day anyway, and it'll be easier if he calls after he doesn't have anything else to worry about.

He waits until he's back in his hotel. He had to ride back with Vince, and it's bad enough that Vince has started giving him looks whenever he picks up his phone. It's only a matter of time before he tries to steal it and see who Caleb's calling.

Chris answers even though he called Scott's cell.

"I think I should be offended that you actually tried to avoid me and call his cell phone after I asked you to call."

"I'm more worried about why he let you answer when he knew I was going to call."

Chris sighs, not answering right away, and Caleb can hear him shift around wherever he is.

"Scott's afraid you're gonna be mad at him," Chris says.

"What? Why? Should I be?" Caleb doesn't remember Scott sounding weird when he called to wake Caleb up in the morning, but Caleb *was* half asleep for that.

"No. He's just being Scott. This was bound to happen sooner or later." There's an edge to Chris's voice, a warning that Chris isn't going to let him talk to Scott until he's sure Caleb's going to play nice.

"Just tell me what's going on. Whatever it is." If he doesn't find out, he's going to make up all kinds of shit in his head even though Chris doesn't sound mad, so it's not like Scott got drunk and did something *really* stupid.

"Scott told his mom about you."

"Shit." Caleb thought it was bad enough when his mom figured out the girl in the picture he'd sent her posed naked. At least Joanna had just laughed at him when he called and said she didn't care. Her boyfriend didn't mind if Caleb's mom thought they were dating as long as nothing was really going on. Did this mean he could get her some extra jobs? Of course it was only a few weeks later when Caleb's mom called to let him know that he should stop lying. They'd figured out he was gay a long time ago.

"Yeah."

"Is he okay?"

"I think he will be," Chris chuckles a little and his voice is muffled a little when he says, "He asked if you were okay. I told you it'd be fine."

"So how upset is his mom? She already knew about y'all."

"She's worried. I don't know what she thinks exactly. Probably that this was my idea and I pushed Scott into it. Which I'd like to say, really isn't fair. This was Scott's idea."

"It was?" They've never let him in on those two weeks of silence before they decided to do this and he's never asked.

"Sort of. He suggested it first, but he didn't push me into it or anything," Chris says and pauses for a few seconds. "Are we going to have to talk about this now?"

"No," Caleb laughs. It's not like even Scott could force Chris into something if he didn't want it. "So did he tell her that?"

"Yeah, but we have to go there for dinner tomorrow anyway. Which you are lucky you get to skip, but I'm pretty sure they're going to make you come over as soon as you get here again."

"You know I don't have more than a day off before you go to Europe, right? Can y'all still come up here next week?" It's bad enough that they're going to Europe without him. It will suck even more if he doesn't get to see them before they leave.

"Yeah. We'll be there. Scott told them you couldn't get time off to come meet them, so they know you aren't just avoiding it. They're used to me having a crazy schedule so they get that much, but we'll probably have to make a plan the next time you come to LA. I don't know. We'll figure it out after we go to see his parents tomorrow and try to calm them down. Which you owe me for. I expect whatever kind of sex I want when we get to New York."

"Because that's so different than usual."

"It is. Usually, I expect it and you don't owe me so you get all pushy about it."

"Right. Can I talk to Scott now?" Caleb says, laughing. He does sort of owe Chris though. Maybe by the time he has to meet Scott's parents, it won't be so bad.

"Sure. He was going to take the phone away soon if I didn't hand it over anyway."

"Hey," Scott says when he takes the phone. "Sorry about all this mess. She called, and it just kind of slipped out."

"Scott, I'm not mad. I'm a little worried, but I'm not mad." If it didn't mean that he'd be stuck going to this dinner, he'd wish he was there to kiss Scott and get him to stop worrying. But Chris will take care of that anyway.

"I know you don't want to meet them, but I think they'll love you. They love Chris. They just need to see that we're happy like this," Scott says. Caleb wonders if he's trying to convince Caleb or just himself.

"It's not a big deal. I'll go meet them. I'm just not sure when I can make it there."

"It's okay. They really are used to Chris having a weird schedule already, and maybe it's better that we go see them without you the first time. That way they'll be less likely to just corner you."

"Yeah. Call me after and tell me how it goes?"

ॐ∞

"YOU'RE quiet," Jessie says when she meets him for lunch the next day.

"It's early. I can barely keep up with what you're saying as it is." Caleb shrugs. It's a fair argument. She should be used to him listening while she chats through lunch.

"You're extra quiet and you look like you didn't sleep at all. Something's wrong." Jessie looks at him and frowns. "Don't tell me they aren't coming. Chris was stupid enough to give me his phone number. They better have a good reason, or I'm calling."

Jessie's more than a foot shorter than Chris. She'd be like a Chihuahua biting at his ankles.

"No, they said they're still coming." Unless they go to see Scott's parents tonight and Scott's parents talk them into breaking up with him.

"Did you fight?"

"Not really."

"Okay, help me out here. Give me something." Jessie leans toward him and reaches across the table. Maybe she could get to Chris. Those little dogs are always kind of scary.

"Scott's parents found out."

"Wow. Do your parents know? Or Chris's?"

"No."

"And they were mad?"

"They weren't happy." Not that he can be surprised about that.

"They knew about Chris and Scott right? Just not about you?" Jessie had gotten most of the story out of him since he'd told her what was going on weeks ago.

"Yeah."

"And you think they're going to talk Scott out of it? Did Scott say that?"

152

"No," Caleb answers. Jessie sighs and motions with her hand for him to go on. "Scott thinks they'll get over it. He and Chris are going to see them tonight to try to calm them down. Scott says they want to meet me next time I come back."

"Okay, so I get why you'd be really nervous about that, but why aren't you trusting Scott? Did Chris say something?"

"He said it'd be fine." But Caleb could tell he wasn't looking forward to this dinner tonight either.

"So really, you're just nervous, and you've talked yourself into the idea that his parents are going to break you up?"

"It's not crazy. You don't know that. They love Chris. He and Scott have been together a long time."

"And they decided that they needed you to really work. You told me yourself that they fought more before you. Besides, I know I've never met Scott, but you've always said he's the most honest one of all of you. Don't you think he would have told you if it was *that* bad?"

"He could be wrong." It's not like Scott has experience with this kind of situation.

"Or you could be over-reacting. I say this because I had to keep distracting Chris while he was here so no one else would notice the way he looked at you. There is no way that man is breaking up with you, and considering that Scott texts all day and I've seen some of the mushy stuff he says? He isn't either."

ഇരു

WHEN Scott calls the next night, Caleb takes it as a good sign. If it went really bad, Chris would be calling.

"How'd it go?" Caleb asks.

"Chris says I owe him whatever sex he wants, too, but it wasn't really that bad. He's just mad because my mom cornered him after dinner. He won't even tell me what they talked about, but it can't be that bad because they still like him, and they seem okay with you. They just made me promise ten times that I'd bring you to meet them when you had time."

"They're really okay?" His parents wouldn't be okay. Well, they were okay when they asked him if Chris and Scott were together, and they were okay when he was with Damian, but that happened after some effort. This would be a whole new issue for his dad to avoid.

"Yeah. They just want me to be happy, and they do love Chris, but they were worried when we got back together. I think they might actually see why it works better with all three of us. Mostly, they were just worried that we weren't really happy."

"Should I be worried about Chris?" Chris refusing to talk wasn't new to him, but Caleb knew that Scott could usually make it happen.

"I don't know. I'll try again tonight. He's lying down in the bedroom claiming to have a headache. You wanna talk to him?"

"Should I?" Chris when he was in a bitchy mood could go a lot of bad ways.

"He probably wants to bitch at you too. It's better to let him do it now or he'll bitch about you avoiding him." Scott chuckles over the line, so it can't be that bad.

"Yeah. You think after y'all come up here, we can fuck it out of him and he'll be over it?"

"Probably," Scott says just before Caleb hears a door open and close. "Hey, you wanna talk to Caleb?"

Scott's voice is low, and Caleb wonders if Chris really did get a migraine out of all this.

"Hey, darlin'," Chris mumbles into the phone. "*You* owe me a lot of sex."

"That bad?" Caleb can't argue. He's hoping between both of them he can avoid getting cornered by himself when he meets Scott's parents.

"You both better be worth it," Chris answers and Caleb can hear Scott's soft laugh in the background.

"You having doubts?" Caleb's sure of the answer, but he can't help asking.

"Man, I'm not fucking going over this with you. I already had to sit and talk about this shit enough today."

CHAPTER 19

"YOU'VE been thinking too much this week, haven't you?" Scott asks. Chris is already asleep behind him, and Caleb's surprised he didn't fall asleep as soon as Chris pulled out. Sex however Chris wants is always some kind of acrobatic adventure. Someday, one of them is going to pull a muscle. It better be Chris.

"I'm okay."

Scott and Chris had said everything was fine a million times in the week before they made it to New York, but that didn't mean he could help considering that they might not show up or they might just come to break it off in person.

"Caleb, we're not going to back out that easy. You need to stop thinking we're going to change our minds. We love you. I thought you got that last time you were in LA." Scott smirks. "It ended up being sort of a big event."

Caleb groans and looks away. Yes, he gets it. He needs to stop freaking out and thinking they're going to break up with him. They haven't done anything to deserve it.

Plus, it makes him look like he has self-esteem issues.

"I know. I'm okay." Lying in his hotel room with Chris wrapped around him and Scott's legs tangled in his, the whole thing seems really stupid.

"Do I need to say it more? Or Chris? It's really not *that* hard to make Chris say it, and I don't really give a shit. I just haven't said it because you seem to take it about as well as he does."

"I do not. I'm better than Chris. I can say I love you." Caleb likes to think he's not that closed off. Not that he doesn't love Chris, but Scott doesn't need another Chris. Actually, the whole planet doesn't need another Chris. "But no, it's not that. I don't need Chris to say it more. You can, if you want, but it's not a big deal. I'm fine."

"All right, but I might have to say it more until you get it into your head. I won't put it on Chris yet though."

"Whatever." Caleb shrugs, reaching behind Scott's neck to pull him in for a kiss. "Sleep now okay? Stop taking advantage of me being too fucked out to hide shit. I know your stupid tricks."

Scott chuckles, but at least he nods, kissing Caleb before turning on his back. "I love you. Start believing it."

"I love you too. See? I'm not fucking Chris."

"Actually, you are fucking Chris."

"Shut up and go to sleep. Tomorrow, you're gonna get fucked too hard to talk after."

ℰℛ

CALEB brings Scott to work with him and leaves Chris in bed. Chris says seven a.m. is too early to get up for a job that isn't his.

Jessie jumps up when they come into her trailer.

157

"Well you're just adorable. I'm Jessie. Caleb better have talked about me."

"Yeah. He did." Scott answers, looking down and blushing as he does, which doesn't really help with the adorable issue. Most people realize that a guy probably doesn't want to be called adorable out loud. Jessie isn't most people.

"Do you have thing for long hair or something?" Jessie tilts her head as she looks at Caleb. "Though I have to admit, they *both* make it look really damn hot and I don't usually like long hair on guys."

"It's a coincidence. I don't have a *thing*." Caleb rolls his eyes, sitting in the makeup chair. "Don't you have a job to do?"

"I'm just going to assume you're bitchy because they didn't let you sleep much last night." Jessie smirks and starts sorting through her makeup. She's got models coming in soon. He should have tried to time it so someone would be there when they came in so she'd have to act like she was just meeting any one of his friends.

"I'm only friends with you because Chris is a possessive freak and I need you to keep that a secret."

"Whatever. You were friends with me before that. Stop bitching while I work," Jessie says even though she's not really doing much that he can see. "You'd think he'd be in a better mood with you here. Maybe you should step outside and call him. That usually cheers him up."

❧❧

FOUR days isn't long enough when he had to work one of those days, and it's even worse that he has to go to work while they go to the airport. Chris is right that it's easier to say goodbye in the hotel, and he'll see them in less than two weeks anyway, but it seems

158

worse. They're not just going back to LA. They're getting on a plane to England, and he can't go with them.

"Hey." Scott wraps his arms around Caleb's waist and leans in for a kiss. "I'll be back in a few days; then you've got some time off. We'll hang out in New York and I'll make you show me around before we go home."

"Yeah." Time off would sound better if he didn't know it was going to have to start with meeting Scott's parents.

"My parents will love you. They're really excited you're staying for Thanksgiving too." When Caleb just nods, Scott pulls him into hug. "I'll call you from London. I'll e-mail you and we love you. Stop freaking out."

"I'm not freaking out." It's just that they didn't let him sleep much at all and it's starting to wear on him.

"Fucking hell. It's a couple weeks. Both of y'all need to stop acting like girls." Chris slides between them and pulls them both into a kiss, dragging it out until Scott gives up and pulls back so they can breathe. Chris kisses him a moment longer before pulling away with a smirk.

"We'll see you in a few days, so don't snap at that pretty little makeup artist so much that she calls me and complains."

ℬℭ

"IT's six in morning. *In England.* I was expecting to wake you up," Chris says when Caleb gets outside the bar so he can hear something besides the music. "Why does it sound like you're in a bad VH1 remix?"

"I just went out with a few people to celebrate the end of fashion week. They picked the bar."

159

"Define a few people."

"Jessie, her boyfriend Drake, some of the models, and some people from *Chic*."

"Models?"

"All male. All gay. Underwear models," Caleb says. Chris deserves it.

"It was just a question. Maybe you can set one of them up with Drake." Chris laughs, giving Caleb some hope for development before he adds, "So who's there from *Chic*?"

Caleb's done his best to sugar-coat Vince. Not because Chris has anything to worry about. It's just that Vince has some boundary issues that Caleb hasn't figured out how to conquer without explaining that one of his boyfriends gets jealous. He's not even sure Vince is gay. Because he hugs every model after every shoot, and he puts his arm around Jessie at least as much as he does Caleb. Jessie thinks he's worried for nothing, and Vince is just an affectionate person. So there's nothing to worry about and he hasn't actually lied to Chris.

"Yes. Vince is here," Caleb says. There's no point in making Chris ask. It's not like Chris has a problem with asking all the time anyway. "No, he hasn't taken off all his clothes and jumped on me."

"It's not that I don't trust you," Chris says. "It's that I don't trust him."

"You haven't actually met him."

"I know people, and all they tell me is that he likes to hug."

"Did you really call when you knew it was late here just to harass me about Vince or did you have a better reason? Did Scott get on the plane and everything?" Scott would kill them both if they argued so much that he ended up sitting around the airport.

"Yeah, but the plane's an hour late."

"Thanks."

"Yeah." Chris is silent a few seconds before he adds. "I do trust you. I'd just feel better if you told him."

"I don't want to just claim one of you, and I'm not working with him after today. So just stop worrying, okay?" Sure, maybe he'd liked hanging out with Vince a little, but it wasn't worth the drama if Vince started asking questions.

"For the record, I'm taking this much better than anyone expected me to. Scott thought I was going to fly back there and kill him yesterday. He was right in your face," Chris says.

"Because you could tell that over the phone."

"I could. His voice was as clear as yours. You should be proud I haven't gotten his number."

"I'll try to remember that." Caleb wishes he didn't have a point, but Chris has overheard Vince inviting him places three or four times, and he hasn't lost it yet. It probably helps that until now, he's always turned Vince down.

"And you'll thank me properly when I get home?"

"After two weeks? I don't think that's really a question."

ℂℂ

SCOTT looks even worse than Caleb expected when he stumbles to the baggage claim with his guitar. Caleb takes the guitar out of his hand, and he leans into Caleb, pressing his face into Caleb's neck.

"Chris didn't let you sleep last night?" Caleb asks, combing through his hair and pressing a kiss on the top of his head.

"He did." Scott steps back and moves to the baggage claim. "I think I'm sick."

161

"You *think* you're sick?"

"I threw up on the plane," Scott says, finding a bench where he can sit down.

Caleb nods, reaching down to rub Scott's back until he has to pull Scott's duffle off the carousel.

Scott's slow on the walk to the cab, struggling to keep up with Caleb even with Caleb carrying everything. When Caleb finally climbs in the cab with him, Scott's leaning against the dirty window with his eyes closed.

"Hey. Come here." Caleb eases him over until Scott's head is resting in his lap.

"Thanks." Scott sighs, dozing as Caleb combs through his hair.

ⳗⳗ

"Sorry," Scott mumbles after washing out his mouth and stumbling back to the bed.

"Sorry for getting sick? Babe, I didn't really think you did it on purpose." Caleb helps Scott strip off his shirt and pulls the blanket up around him.

"Still not what you were looking forward to."

"I was looking forward to seeing you," Caleb says, climbing into bed and pulling Scott against him. "And you're here."

"Missed you too." Scott grins as he snuggles into Caleb's side.

"Tell me if you need anything?"

"I'm never going to be able to be sick without you again."

"You'd have Chris." Caleb tries not to think about how that'd end up happening.

162

Scott just chuckles. "I'm lucky if Chris pays Jason ten bucks to bring me chicken soup."

"What?"

"He's scared of sick people. And germs. And getting sick himself."

"So he just disappears?" Caleb wants to be angry at Chris on Scott's behalf, but Scott just laughs.

"Forcing him isn't worth it. It's worse if he actually gets sick himself."

"That bad?"

"It's easier to take care of my nephew when he's sick. Aiden's *four*. Chris might as well be a whiney three-year-old."

"I'm not sure if I want to see that or not."

"I'm just glad I won't have to do it by myself anymore."

ॐ☙

"BUT he's just regular sick, right? Not in the hospital or anything?" Chris asks when Caleb explains why he doesn't want to wake Scott up for the phone.

"It's probably just a virus that'll be over in a couple days." If it's not, Caleb will start worrying and take him to a doctor, but for now there's no reason for Chris to fly to New York and get in the way.

"And you're still sleeping in the bed with him?"

"I'm not making out with him. I'm not going to catch a stomach virus from him breathing on me." It's stupid, and he should be mad about finding out that Chris probably won't ever be nursing him back to health either, but it's always nice to find another gap in their relationship that he can fill.

"You're both going to be sick when I get back." Chris sighs like he's the one suffering.

"We'll be fine."

"You say that now."

Scott stirs next him. His eyes blink open as he turns to press his face into Caleb's stomach.

"Chris?" Scott looks up at him, and his hand lifts a few inches.

"Scott's awake. Sort of. You want me to give him the phone or are you afraid it will transmit his germs across the Atlantic?"

Scott chuckles as Chris groans over the phone. "Shut up, and give him the phone."

"Hey. Caleb has to stay. I'm spoiled now," Scott says when he takes the phone. Caleb wishes he could hear whatever Chris says that makes Scott smile and glance up at Caleb before he answers. "You know Jason wants to have your brain examined, right?"

❧❦

WHEN Vince calls two days later, Scott's well enough to comment.

"What'd he want you to do?"

"Some kind of dinner party. He thought I was just staying in town because the job ended early. I told him a friend was visiting."

"And he didn't want to invite me?" Scott asks like it's normal to just add people onto an invitation. Maybe it is because Vince *did* just that.

"He did. I just thought you wouldn't want to."

"You thought I wouldn't want to or that it would be a problem?" Scott reaches out so he can take Caleb's hand and pull him closer. Scott pulls until Caleb's straddling his lap, knees resting on the bed.

"He's not like our other friends." Vince is loud where Jason's quiet and he goes for the full hug instead of the quick half handshake man-hug.

"But you like him? As a friend. I'm not Chris. You're allowed to have your own friends." Scott wraps both arms around his waist and rubs the small of his back until he relaxes in Scott's lap.

"Chris already hates him."

"Chris hasn't met him. He hated you when I started talking about you." Scott grins and pecks a quick kiss on his lips.

"I don't like Vince like that." For one thing, he doesn't want to try to fit anyone else in the bed.

Scott laughs. "Good. Because you're special. Chris isn't going to share that much. But he can deal with you having a friend. He just isn't going to like Vince as much as he ended up liking you—not that he didn't try like hell to hate you"

"So why'd he give me a chance?" Even Jason's still confused about why Chris didn't just kick his ass instead.

"He couldn't really get mad about me falling for you when he was doing the same thing."

Caleb can feel his face get hot, but when he tries to get up, Scott tightens his hold and leans in to kiss his neck. Scott waits until he relaxes before speaking again. If he's lucky, it won't be mushy.

"So why don't you call him back and tell him we'll go. I can meet him and tell Chris he's nothing to worry about."

ॐ

VINCE hugs him as soon as he opens the door, and then he smiles, introduces himself to Scott and hugs him too.

"How are you friends with this guy?" Vince asks, still looking at Scott. "Is there a secret? Because he turns me down most of the time."

"He got too drunk at a bar and my friend brought him home. He was obligated," Scott answers.

"Hey! I'm friendly," Caleb said, pushing Vince a little. Maybe it would be better if he'd brought Chris. Growling at Vince might be better than teaming up with him. "I was nice to you at work."

"You were helpful. Which I appreciated," Vince says.

"Sorry." If he wasn't so worried about Chris freaking out, maybe he would have been nicer.

"You weren't mean, just very professional. Kind of guarded. I believe the drunk thing though. You were much cooler when I got you to drink." Vince winks at Scott as a pretty brunette ducks under his arm. She looks familiar and Caleb's pretty sure she modeled in one of his spreads a couple years ago. Vince leans down to kiss the top of her head.

"Are you being mean to my guests?" she asks, though her attempt to glare at Vince doesn't really hold.

"I invited them! They're mine." Vince looks down, giving her full on puppy eyes.

"I cooked. All guests are mine. Play nice." She leans up to kiss him before turning to Scott. "I'm Marissa. Vince's girlfriend. Isn't he lucky I put up with him forgetting to introduce me?"

Scott sends him a smirk like he should have figured this out on his own before turning to Marissa and introducing himself.

"I was going to introduce you," Vince breaks in. "Caleb, this is my girlfriend Marissa. She would have come with us last weekend, but she was modeling in Paris. I'm amazingly lucky to have her because she's so hot and cool and amazing."

"Better." Marissa gives Vince a nod of approval before grabbing onto Scott and pulling him toward the dining room. Vince smiles, his eyes following her with the same kind of lovesick gaze Jason gives to his girlfriend.

"She really is awesome. You'll love her." Vince throws his arm around Caleb to guide him to the dining room, and Caleb doesn't bother worrying about his intentions. So Vince is just affectionate. He's got a girlfriend. Chris can get over it.

CHAPTER 20

CHRIS and Scott are way too calm as they get out of Scott's car in front of Scott's parents house.

"Relax, darlin'. The worst happened before you were here. They're all right." Chris stands at his right as Scott opens the door.

"Come on. They never hear me come in." Scott reaches back and threads their fingers together to pull him inside. They've never held hands before. Hell, it's not something he usually does at all. It's not like he's going to walk down the street holding hands with a guy, but he doesn't hate it when Scott squeezes his hand.

"Hey, sweetie." Scott's mom comes into the foyer to great them, followed by his dad, and Scott lets go of his hand to hug his parents. It's stupid, but he wants Scott's hand back already.

"Caleb, right?" Scott's mom smiles at him, taking his hand and holding it for a moment instead of just shaking it. That's okay. Shaking hands always feels awkward anyway. The less he has to do it, the better.

"Yes, ma'am. It's nice to meet you."

"You too." She smiles and lets him go so he can shake hands with Scott's dad. He nods to Caleb, and Caleb tries to smile even though he feels like he's in high school. That was probably the last time he met parents this way.

Chris gets hugs from them both because he's Chris and not some new guy who stepped in the middle of a relationship they probably liked just fine before.

"Come on, dinner's about ready. Scott, go set the table for me?"

Caleb thinks for a second that he's about to get left alone and he's going to say something stupid, but Scott takes his hand again and pulls him into the kitchen. "Come on. You get to help."

He really doesn't mind setting the table if it means he doesn't get left with Scott's parents.

"Chris is going to be pissed." Caleb's not sure if he really needs to be whispering, but it's got to be better to be safe.

"He'll be okay. They don't have much left to drill him for anyway. We just agreed to make sure you didn't end up alone with them."

"You actually discussed a plan and didn't tell me?" Scott hands him plates. Plates are good because there's no way he can remember where the silverware is supposed to go right now.

"It wasn't really a discussion. We thought it was obvious that we weren't going to leave you alone." Scott offers him a small smile as he finishes the last place setting. "Don't worry. Dinner's easy and then we'll just hang out."

Hang out? They were just going to hang out? Because that wasn't going to be weird and awkward.

ᔆᐤ�03

HANGING out apparently meant family game night. With board games. Caleb hasn't played a board game since church camp, but maybe anything is better than just sitting around and trying to talk. Chris and Scott covered for his lack of interesting dinner conversation, but if they had to just sit around in the living room and talk, his continual stumbling through conversation would probably make them think he couldn't speak without a script. At least now he can lean down and play with the dog when he runs out of things to say.

So maybe family game night isn't the worst thing in the world. It's just weird to watch Chris and Scott argue over if they're playing Trivial Pursuit or Cranium.

"You only want to play Trivial Pursuit because you always win," Scott says.

"So? Who wants to play a game they lose?" Chris asks, like this should make everyone else want to play too.

"We don't always lose at Cranium. And it's not boring." Is Cranium a team game? It can't be a partner game unless Scott hasn't realized just how much that would make Caleb look like the third wheel.

"I didn't say it was boring. I just said Trivial Pursuit is better."

"I know. *I'm* saying Trivial Pursuit is boring."

"Sixty seconds and we're playing Scrabble," Scott's dad says.

They both turn to look at him even though they haven't cared what he said before. He might as well not even have been sitting between them before now.

"I really don't care," he says because he really fucking *doesn't.*

"Have you played Cranium before?" Chris asks.

"No."

"Dude, it's a team game. He might suck," Chris tells Scott.

"Fine. Trivial Pursuit. Where I will lose for sure." Scott rolls his eyes, but he laughs when Chris celebrates his victory. "But I'm training Caleb at Cranium and we're playing Cranium next time."

Scott leans back on the couch and wraps an arm around his shoulders. "Please beat him so he won't want to play anymore."

℘〇℘

CALEB'S ninety percent sure that the only reason Chris isn't pouting about losing the game is the look Scott's mom gave him when he started glaring. He's pretty sure he also heard her whisper something about calling his mama. Caleb just hopes she's not going to do that, because he needs a while before he has to do this with Chris's parents. He never considered he'd have to do all the awkward parts of a relationship twice.

"We expect all three of you back for Thanksgiving unless you change your minds and make it back to see your families." Scott's mom hugs Chris and he can see her lips move close to Chris's ear, but he can't make out the words. Then she does the last thing Caleb expects and turns around to hug *him*.

"We're happy as long as he's happy," she whispers, squeezing him before pulling away to hug Scott.

When they get to Caleb's SUV, Caleb tosses Scott the keys to drive. Chris takes the front seat and leaves Caleb to slide into the back. He's quiet as they pull out of the driveway, leaving Caleb to wonder if there's something more he's upset about than losing a stupid board game.

"Stop pouting." Scott's eyes don't leave the road as he reaches over to poke Chris in the side. "You're going to make him think you're really mad. If he goes back to his apartment, I'm blaming you."

"I'm not pouting," Chris mumbles even though it's clear he is.

"Move to the back and be nice."

"Or what?"

"I'll make you play Taboo when it's my turn to choose."

Chris sighs and moves to the backseat. "So what'd she say when she was hugging you?"

"That they're happy as long as Scott's happy. What'd she say to you?" Chris still isn't touching him.

"That I had to take care of you both because she knows you're worse than little princesses who get birds to braid their hair." Chris smirks and slides down to slouch in the bench seat.

"That's not what she said."

"It's what she should've said." Chris elbows him and then lets his hand settle on Caleb's thigh for the rest of the trip.

CHAPTER 21

CALEB is about to give up on getting into LA fashion week when he gets a call from *Mod* two days before the first show.

"One of interns said she saw you working in New York. One of our main photographers went diva on us and is refusing to shoot the event. They refused to give her girlfriend a chance to show her ugly line of jeans or something. Are you free?"

He wishes he could play hardball, but he's not such a big name that he can just sit around and wait for artistic offers. Besides, he likes fashion week even though he's not going to admit it to Chris.

"*Mod*, huh?" Chris says when he finds out. "You think they might want you full time?"

Chris is even less subtle when he's trying. For a guy who refuses to get rid of his own apartment and move in with Scott, he's determined to get some sign that Caleb's not going to spend a lot more time out of LA.

"No idea. Could just be a one time thing. I'm just glad I got something."

Chris nods, not commenting as he runs his hand over Caleb's bare chest.

"You guys are awake before coffee?" Scott asks, coming in the door balancing three mugs.

"Caleb's fault."

"I'm sorry *Mod* thinks ten o'clock is an okay time to call on a Thursday."

"*Mod?*" Scott sits on Caleb's other side, back propped up against the headboard.

"Their photographer's issues are my gain. I've got a job."

"Chris is shooting an ad campaign. You're shooting LA Fashion Week. I'm looking like the slacker."

"You have a show next weekend," Chris says.

"You date Chris. Full time job." Caleb leans toward Scott, trying not to spill his coffee as Chris tries to swat him.

"You're the one throwing hissy fits when you don't get enough attention," Chris laughs, and Caleb only doesn't kill him because they both have coffee and they just changed the sheets.

"Never mind. You're both full time jobs. I should be paid overtime."

੪つCR

CALEB'S never worked LA fashion week before, and he doesn't have any inside connections like he does in New York. Of course, he's not going to say that to the people from *Mod* when they're too hurried to do more than push a list of shows they want pictures from, and a list of designers they want to feature.

So of course the first person he sees when he walks in is Damian.

174

It's not that he wants Damian back. He has two boyfriends and they're both better to him than Damian ever was. It's just that he'd like to see Damian fat and lonely instead of hot and leaning close to the first designer Caleb needs to talk to.

"Hey! When *Chic* sent me here, I thought I wouldn't be seeing you until I could get some time off." Vince's arm drapes over his shoulders, and his smile draws Caleb away from Damian.

"I'm with the enemy." Caleb holds up the *Mod* press pass.

"I'm sure we can still rise above that and get along." Vince nods, faking seriousness before giving up and laughing.

"Somehow we'll make it work."

"So are you supposed to get extra shots of Michael Balles's line like I am?"

"Yeah."

"So why aren't you beating me to it?"

Caleb shrugs. He's not even sure if anyone told Vince he's gay, and he's not in the mood for Vince to jump away from him like he has the plague.

"Which one?" Vince asks.

"What?"

"Okay, please don't hit me if I'm wrong, but you're gay, right?" Vince pulls away just enough to get a better look at his face.

"Yeah. I wasn't sure you knew."

"There were a few hints." Vince nods to where Damian is still talking to Michael. "So which one's your ex? If it's Michael, I'm going to guess he broke up with you because you told him the truth that his spring line was a disaster."

"Other one."

"You want me to pretend to be your hot new boyfriend?"

175

"No." Caleb laughs, elbowing Vince in the side.

"What? I'm hot! He'd be very jealous."

"Because I'm over him anyway. I don't care. I just don't want to deal with him."

"Okay, so how about I go over there and chase him away? Then we can get our stuff done together."

"You're really bad at this rival magazines thing," Caleb says, but he must be too because he already knows he's going to spend the whole day with Vince if he can.

𝔰𝔬 ❧

ON FRIDAY, Caleb's SUV won't start. The lights won't come on and even Caleb knows enough about cars to know that the battery is probably dead. He's pulling out his phone to call Chris when Vince stops him.

"I've got cables in my truck." Vince runs off to move his truck, leaving Caleb to pocket his phone and get in his car. Maybe if he just pops the hood and sits in his car, Vince won't notice that he doesn't remember how to hook up the cables. His brother showed him years ago, but it's been a long time since he was distracted enough to leave his lights on.

Vince smirks, but he doesn't say anything as he clips the cables to the battery and starts his truck.

"Okay. Try it."

Caleb turns the key and nothing happens. Vince shrugs and tries again, this time waiting a bit longer before he tells Caleb to try again. Still nothing.

"Are you sure you're doing it right?" Caleb asks. He doesn't know any better, but he's sure Chris does.

176

"Yeah. It's not like it works every time," Vince laughs, shrugging like it's not such a big deal. "Come on. I'll take you home, and you can call to have it towed or something."

He almost gives Vince directions to Scott's place instead of his own, but Chris is probably there, and the last thing he needs is Chris giving Vince the third degree before Caleb has even explained who the hell Chris is.

"Call me if you need a ride tomorrow. Marissa's apartment is right around here anyway," Vince says when he pulls in front of Caleb's building.

"Sure," Caleb says even though he knows what Chris will have to say about that.

꿍꿍

BY THE end of the week, he has everything *Mod* could ever want. Maybe they'll even let him replace the flakey photographer who got him this job.

"Let's go out," Vince says as he leads the way to his car. He turns around and walks backward as he talks. "I'll call Marissa. You can call someone if you want and we'll get wasted."

Chris would just love that. He's already edgy since he found out Vince was in town, and Caleb wasn't fooled in the morning when Chris offered to drive him instead of letting him call Vince. "Thanks, but I think I'll pass."

"Come on. If you don't go, I'm going to have a complex about you hating me again."

"You never had a complex," Caleb laughs, punching Vince in the arm. Vince pretends he's actually hurt, his lips turning into the worst pout Caleb's ever seen.

"I can *give* him a damn complex." Chris steps out from behind Vince's rental SUV. Shit.

"Whoa. Calm down now," Vince says, holding up his hands and giving Caleb a confused look. Probably because Caleb never mentioned a boyfriend and now there's a crazy jealous one getting in his face.

"I'll calm down when you get out of here and stay away from him." Chris reaches out to grab Caleb's arm as he glares at Vince, but Caleb moves out of his reach.

"He doesn't have to stay away. I'm allowed to have friends."

"Friends? He was asking you out!"

"He was asking me to go hang out with him and his *girlfriend.*"

"Didn't look like that. So he says he's got a girlfriend? That doesn't mean he's not hoping to hook up with you too." Chris reaches for him again, but Caleb pulls away, only making Chris angrier. "What? You want to go home with him instead now?"

"You're fucking insane. I'll get a ride home from Vince. You can call me if you get some sense. You can't fucking tell me who to be friends with."

"You're going to go with *him*?"

"Well, I'm not going with you. I'm not your property. Telling my friends to stay away from me isn't going to get you laid." Caleb turns away, walking around to the passenger side. Vince nods to him, but Caleb doesn't miss that he doesn't turn his back to Chris as he opens the door and slides in.

Vince doesn't say anything. He just nods when Caleb gives him directions. It's creepy. Vince hasn't been silent since Caleb met him.

"You could've told me you had a boyfriend," Vince says when he stops the SUV. He doesn't insert the word crazy, but it's there in his voice.

"It's complicated."

"Are you gonna be okay?"

Caleb shrugs, looking out the window to try to avoid the looks Vince keeps throwing his way.

"That doesn't make me want to leave you here alone."

"He's not abusive or anything. Yes, I know everyone says that, but he's not. It's not like I couldn't take him myself if he was." He really doesn't need Vince to protect him anyway. He's gay, not helpless.

"Not what I was worried about, but now I kind of am."

"It'll be fine," Caleb says. Scott will tell Chris he's an idiot and they'll have make-up sex.

"You don't sound too sure about that," Vince says as Caleb climbs out of the truck.

"We've never fought like this before." They've argued and snapped at each other, but it's never been so bad that he thinks he's not going to end up with Chris wrapped around him at the end of the night.

CHAPTER 22

SCOTT shows up two hours after Vince leaves. He doesn't knock. He just walks in, pulls Caleb off the couch, and into his arms. "He'll figure out he fucked up, babe. You just gotta give him some time to cool off."

"You talked to him?"

"Yeah. Then I yelled some." Scott sits down on the couch, tugging Caleb against him. "He's done this with me before."

"Over who?" The last time Caleb checked Scott didn't have a lot of friends he didn't share with Chris.

"Danielle."

"Danielle?"

"Sometimes he's stupid," Scott says and Caleb doesn't argue.

"And he came back and apologized?"

"Well, I got pissed off and broke up with him," Scott admits. "And I might have thrown some things."

"*You* threw things? If we fight, are you going to throw things at me?"

"Not unless I think we're breaking up."

"That's not helping me." Caleb elbows him, but doesn't move out of his arms. It's just that Scott is usually better at this.

"It only lasted four months," Scott says like four months isn't a long time to be broken up.

"And *then* he apologized?"

"Then Jason locked us in a hotel room and our friends each paid for a room around us so no one would complain about the noise we made banging on the door and yelling at them. Chris apologized the third day. We didn't tell Jason we made up until the sixth." Scott grins and leans down to kiss his forehead.

"This can't take four months," Caleb shakes his head. "You can't just go between us until he gets some sense."

"I know, but I think we can make it a day while he cools off. Then I can talk to him. He knows he's wrong anyway."

"If he knows he's wrong, then why the fuck isn't he already over here?" It's not like he wouldn't let Chris in.

"He's scared, and he's going to have to admit that when he apologizes. He hates admitting he's scared ten times more than he hates apologizing."

"He's scared?"

"That you'll leave us." Scott stops him before he can argue. "I know it's stupid. I've been telling him that for weeks, but he hasn't met Vince and you've spent the whole week with him. He picked you up and brought you home three times. Chris is just terrified you'll leave, and he can't admit that. He spent all day today fixing your car so he could take it to you."

"He did?"

"You didn't see it?" Scott's hand stops stroking his arm.

"I didn't have a chance. He just came out of nowhere and started yelling at Vince."

181

"And you're sure it didn't look worse than it was?" Scott asks. At least he takes Caleb's hand and laces their fingers together.

"*You've* met Vince! And I've told Chris over and over that it's not like that."

"I said he was scared. I never said he wasn't a bit slow."

Caleb sighs, relaxing in Scott's arms as Scott traces patterns over his stomach.

"You're not sleeping here, are you?" Caleb asks.

"No. But Chris isn't sleeping at my place either. It wouldn't be right."

Caleb nods, leaning back against Scott's chest and enjoying him while he's still there.

℘ℭℛ

WHEN Chris comes over the next day, Scott is right behind him.

"Did Scott make you come over?" Caleb wants to make up. He doesn't want Chris to apologize just because Scott made him.

"No, Scott didn't *make* me do anything. I just thought he had a right to be here considering he's in this relationship too." Chris pushes past him into the apartment. It's funny how Chris apologizing doesn't seem all that different from fighting with him in the first place.

"It's okay," Scott says before Caleb can say anything. "Just try with him, okay? Just try."

Caleb nods because Chris is right. This whole thing affects Scott just as much as them.

182

Chris waits until Caleb and Scott sit on the couch before sitting across from them on the loveseat. He just stares at his hands for a minute before looking at Scott and then Caleb.

"I overreacted." Chris looks at Scott again, and Caleb can see Scott nod out of the corner of his eye. He wonders how long it's going to take before Chris trusts him the way he trusts Scott.

"Yeah."

"He still shouldn't be all over you like that."

"He wasn't all over me. He had his arm around my shoulders. You're all over Jason more than that."

"You know Jason. Jason's like my little brother. He'd make friends with every murderer that walked around on the streets if I didn't watch out for him."

"And I get that. So you should get that I need other friends."

"You have friends," Chris says. Scott must have given him a look because he changes course before Caleb can get mad, but it's stilted like he's forcing every word out. "Okay, I get that you can have friends that aren't our friends, but if you're going to be going out to bars with him, he should have known you're not single. All my friends know we're together. The guys at the studio even know I'm not single."

"Half of them think you're still just with Scott."

"I'm working on that. You *know* that." Chris looks at Scott. It's not hard to read them at all anymore. This look says it's not his fault anymore if Caleb's not trying.

"He knows I'm not single now." When he looks at Scott to point out that he *is* trying, Scott just rolls his eyes and points him back to Chris.

"He doesn't know about Scott. You're hanging out enough that he should know about Scott," Chris says, glancing at Scott when he says it.

"I can't just tell him that. I didn't want him to only know about one of you, and that's why he didn't know anything."

"If he's gonna be your friend, then you should be able to tell him. If he gives a shit, then you're not gonna be able to be friends with him anyway." Chris bites his lip and looks at Scott again. "Unless you don't plan on being with us long enough for it to matter."

"Chris. That's not it. Of course I plan on being with you, both of you. I just need more time to tell him."

"Why? So it's worse if he freaks out, or so you spend all this time worrying about it when he doesn't care?"

Caleb can't come up with a decent argument for that. He can't admit that he just doesn't want to deal with it because if Vince freaks out, he's back to not having any friends in LA outside of Chris or Scott. Sure, Vince spends half his time in New York, but he spends the other half in LA visiting Marissa. Chris gets up and walks over to sit next him.

"Jessie was okay with it. He might be okay. But he should know, and we should be able to meet him."

"Technically you've both already met him," Caleb says. Scott reaches over and taps his leg. "Okay. I know what you mean. Just give me a little time to figure it out."

"A little," Chris repeats.

"Are you going to make me set a date?" It's not fair considering that Vince is only going to be in LA a few more days.

"No, but if you want us to meet him with other people around, you could just invite him to Jason's show."

"True. He'll require a public place to be around you again. I had to convince him you weren't actually crazy and he didn't need to call an intervention to get me out of an abusive relationship."

"I said I was sorry about that."

"No you didn't. You just admitted you overreacted."

"Fine. I'm sorry." Chris sighs when Caleb rolls his eyes. When he speaks again, his tone is softer. "I'm sorry. I know I overreacted, and I'm sorry that I got so upset. Can we have makeup sex now?"

"That's all you think about," Caleb laughs. As long as he doesn't have to sleep alone again, he can put up with whatever weird way Chris wants to have sex.

"Come on. You'll like my makeup sex. You get to pick whatever you want." Chris smirks and stands, pulling Caleb up with him.

"I suggest picking something he doesn't usually wanna do," Scott says. "Because he means it when he says whatever you want."

"Scott always picks the same thing. It makes me think he has a complex about getting fucked—even though he begs for it every time."

"Scott picks fucking you?" It's not like they can't urge Chris into it when they really want it.

"In missionary. It's so boring that he's blushing because I'm telling you."

"Asshole." Scott buries his face in the back of Caleb's neck and pushes him toward the bedroom.

"Come on. You don't want to be doing just that when you piss him off, do you?"

"I don't know. Depends on what you want." Chris slips his hands under Caleb's shirt, pulling it up and over his head.

There's only one thing Caleb can think of and he sure as hell isn't asking for it. It's not really the kind of thing you ask for.

"Am I really gonna have to pry this out of you?" Chris asks, pressing up against him. He leans down, licking a stripe up Caleb's neck and moving up to nibble at his ear. "Are you gonna make me guess?"

Scott reaches around, unbuttoning both of their jeans and pushing all the clothes away. "You should take advantage. He won't even make you beg right now."

Caleb lets them push him on the bed and press against him from each side. Scott kisses him long and slow until Chris turns his head to claim Caleb's mouth.

"So, darlin', what do you want?" Chris kisses down his neck, and lets his hands roam over Caleb's body as he talks. "I know you like to be fucked. You like to ride me, but you like it more when you're on your side and Scott can suck you off. I'm sure he wouldn't mind helping me out with that. That what you want?"

Caleb doesn't answer, even though he thinks that maybe he should just agree with something so Chris will let it drop.

"You wanna fuck me? Want me to ride you? Never done that for you."

It's tempting. Caleb can't help moaning just thinking about it.

"We can do that, but why do I get the idea you want something else more?" Chris glances to where Scott is sucking a bruise into Caleb's hip. Caleb shifts, pushing closer to Scott as Chris keeps talking. "Hum, I do remember something that drove you so crazy that you couldn't concentrate on fucking Scott."

Caleb can't hold in his whimper. He doesn't really want to anyway. If Chris brings it up, he can't mind doing it that much.

"That's what you want? You want me to lick you open until you come in Scott's mouth?" Chris doesn't wait for an answer. He just pushes Caleb onto his side and kisses down his back.

Scott licks a stripe up his cock as Chris spreads him open and licks down his crack. Chris teases, licking over him, letting the tip of his tongue slip inside just enough for Caleb to shiver and push back against him.

"Pushy." Chris laughs, pulling back and running his finger over the opening.

"I though you said no teasing. Something about making up for you being an idiot."

Chris doesn't answer, but his tongue presses inside, licking and pushing in and out as Caleb pushes into Scott's mouth. It's only minutes before Caleb crumbles under the assault, whimpering and pulling on Scott's hair as he comes.

"You're gonna make me piss you off on purpose," Caleb mumbles as he struggles not to pass out before either of them have gotten off.

CHAPTER 23

CHRIS is watching him when he wakes up the next morning. He only vaguely remembers stumbling to Chris's truck so they could sleep at Scott's.

"Hey." Chris smiles and trails his finger down Caleb's jaw.

"Hey." It's too early. Anytime Scott is still passed out next to him, it's too early. Caleb snuggles closer to Chris and closes his eyes. "Go back to sleep."

When he wakes up again, Scott's gone, and he can smell the coffee brewing. Chris is watching him again.

"You're starting to creep me out with all the staring." Caleb sighs and lets his head rest on Chris's chest.

"Sorry," Chris mumbles. That's not normal.

"I was joking." Caleb looks up at him and he nods. "Is something wrong? Because I really thought I remembered making up."

"Yeah. We're good. I was just thinking." Chris shrugs. "Are you really going to tell him?"

"I told you I would." He's not sure how he's going to do it. Alcohol might have to be involved.

"Invite him to Jason's show and you'll have Jason and Scott to make me be nice."

"Like anyone can actually control you."

ℭℜ

VINCE invites him to Marissa's apartment on Wednesday. Marissa has a night shoot and won't be home until after midnight. Vince says he'll be bored, but Caleb's pretty sure he's just worried that Chris really is some kind of abusive asshole.

"You're going to his apartment?" Chris keeps his voice even, but his tight grip on the arm of the couch gives him away.

"You realize that if you want me to tell him, I do actually have to see him again." Caleb turns on the couch, leaning against the other arm and letting his legs drape over Chris's lap. The water in the kitchen where Scott is washing the dishes shuts off, but he doesn't interrupt.

"You'll tell him tonight?" Chris relaxes, and his hand moves from the arm of the couch to rub Caleb's calf.

"That's the plan."

"Call us if he's not okay."

"Are you going to burst in and kick his ass?"

"Only if you want me to."

ℭℜ

"OKAY. I'm drunk. Why am I drunk?" Vince is lying next to him on floor of Vince's apartment.

189

"Because we drank a lot of vodka." Caleb doesn't even like vodka. He's never gotten drunk off of vodka and not thrown it all up. Maybe he'll be okay this time if he just doesn't move.

"Why did you make me drink a lot of vodka? This is your fault." Vince rolls on his side to face him. "Seriously, dude. You've been trying to tell me something all night. If you're going to confess that you have a huge man-crush on me, then now is the time. I could drink a few more shots and not remember it in the morning."

"I don't have a man-crush on you."

"Then what did you want to tell me? Is something up with Chris? Did he find out about Scott or something?"

"What?"

"Dude. Don't tell me nothing's going on with Scott. I thought he was your boyfriend until I met Chris. You were making eyes at each other the whole dinner party. Marissa went on and on about how cute you were. Now she's upset because she liked Scott and she can't torture me with descriptions of the cuteness."

"So what the hell have you been thinking I'm doing?"

"I don't know! I figured maybe you really liked Scott, but you couldn't break up with Chris because he's all insane and shit."

"Chris isn't insane." Except for the times that he kind of is.

"I thought he was going to kill me for talking to you."

"He apologized for that. In a few ways."

"I really didn't need to know that," Vince says, but he laughs and shoves Caleb's shoulder. "So what's going on then?"

"I'm sort of dating them both."

"Sort of?"

"Okay, I am dating them both. But I'm not cheating. It's not like that."

"How is it not like that?" Vince asks, but it's not accusing.

"They're together too. We're all together." Caleb tries to roll over to get a better look at Vince, but his stomach lurches in protest.

"You're all together. Like at the same time." Vince hasn't kicked him out yet. That has to be a good sign.

"Yeah."

Vince scrunches his face and Caleb is getting ready to hear how gross Vince thinks he is when Vince says, "So how does that work? Do you all line up or something?"

෧ଓ

"Darlin', wake up for me."

Caleb struggles to open his eyes. The last thing he can remember is telling Vince that he wasn't drunk enough to explain his sex life. He really hopes he didn't start talking with the next few shots. Still, none of that explains why Chris is here.

"Why're you here? Did something happen? Were you being creepy and waiting in the parking lot?"

He can hear Vince laughing. Marissa's carpet is digging into his cheek. At least it's soft, girly carpet.

"You called Scott. You said you wanted to sleep at home. I said I'd come get you because he was already asleep."

"Time?" He remembers passing midnight at some point.

"Three. You only called about half an hour ago."

"He passed out right after that," Vince fills in. Vince sucks. Vince let him drink too much.

"You still want me to take you home?" Chris's hand cups his cheek, his thumb stroking down Caleb's jaw.

191

"I can't get up."

Chris chuckles. "I'm not gonna carry you."

Chris is a liar anyway because he slips his arm under Caleb's back and helps him sit up.

"Just help me up. I can walk." Chris lifts him, letting Caleb lean against him as they walk to the door. Chris says something to Vince, but Caleb doesn't understand a thing.

❧

CALEB rolls over as he wakes, hiding his face in Chris's chest to block out the little bit of light that the curtains let through. Chris. How the hell is he in bed with Chris? He sits up too fast and his vision swims.

"Hey, darlin'. Sudden movements are probably a bad idea for you right now." Chris reaches for him and guides him back to the pillow.

"How'd I get here?"

"You called at 2:30 wanting to come home. Scared the shit out of me. I thought he'd reacted badly until you started rambling about wanting to sleep with us—which Vince heard by the way. I guess if that didn't scare him away, he's gonna stick around for you."

"You picked me up?"

"Well, neither of you were fit to drive." Chris rolls his eyes, but Caleb can forgive him because he's also running his fingers through Caleb's hair to ease away his headache. Caleb moves down the bed, resting his head on Chris's stomach.

"You could've let me sleep there. You didn't have to drive half an hour in the middle of the night."

Chris's hand stills in his hair for a second before he shrugs. "Scott would've bitched at me."

"Chris is a big liar. He wanted you home," Scott says, walking in with a glass of water and a bottle of aspirin. "I woke up when he was bringing you in. He had to pretty much carry you, and you were whining about something. You spit water at him when he was trying to make you drink something."

Chris glares at Scott. "If you say it was cute, I'm not letting you fuck me for at least three months."

℘℘℘

"IT'LL be fine. I already like Vince." Scott's fingers brush over the back of his hand in the dim light of the club. Scott's finger links with his for a second before he lets go. Scott doesn't care much about PDA, but here at the club where he and Jason share a lot of the same fans, both he and Chris don't want to be so obvious. Sometimes Caleb wonders what will happen if they ever get signed. He doesn't really want to go back in the closet after six years out of it.

"Chris still doesn't like him."

"Chris doesn't like anyone he doesn't bring into the group himself." Scott smirks as he glances to where Chris is going over Jason's set list. "Just wait until he decides Jason doesn't need him anymore and he picks up a new project. He'll forget about Vince when he finds someone else who has a lot of talent, but isn't making it. He'll bring some new guy into the group himself, and Vince will be old news."

"Why's he gotta have a project?" It's not like they're going to stop hanging out with Jason. There's still things Jason needs help with.

"You're not gonna to be any better when he brings someone in, are you?" Scott laughs, stepping closer to Caleb so he can brush his hand over Caleb's side.

"I'll be okay."

"Sure you will. Just like Chris will be okay when Vince gets here." Scott smiles at his sigh and pulls him back behind the wall leading backstage. Scott plays at the club enough to get away with it. He cups Caleb's cheek and kisses him until he can't help relaxing into it. "Give it time. Chris already saw him again when he picked you up from Vince's apartment, and he didn't pick a fight then. Chris'll get used to him."

Caleb nods and steals another kiss before stepping back into the open floor of the club. Scott has to be right. After all, Chris got used to Danielle and it's not like Vince doesn't have a girlfriend.

"Hey!" Marissa rushed up to them, pulling Vince behind her. "We were starting to think you hadn't recovered enough to show up."

Marissa hugged him, and then Scott before glancing around. "Where's Chris? I still don't believe these rumors that he's scary. He was so sweet when he came to pick you up."

Caleb groans, resisting the urge to hide his face in Scott's neck.

"He's helping Jason set up," Scott fills in when Caleb doesn't answer. "He doesn't believe Jason doesn't need his help anymore."

"Maybe Jason still needs some help." The last thing Caleb needs is Chris picking some new project he doesn't even know.

"I'm really the only sane one," Scott says to Vince. "You just made friends with the other crazy one."

"I'm sane." Caleb shoves him, but he doesn't step away. Chris has spotted Vince, and he's already moving away from Jason. It would be really nice if Danielle would get here and Jason would start playing so they could all stop and pay attention to Jason instead of him.

Chris smiles and takes Marissa's hand first.

"Nice to meet you again when we don't both have wasted boyfriends to pick up off the floor," Marissa says, giggling. At least this time, Vince is blushing with him.

Chris nods, chuckling, but he sobers before shaking hands with Vince.

"Glad you could make it," he says, but Caleb can see how hard he grips Vince's hand before he lets go. His hand hovers over the small of Caleb's back, his possessiveness battling with his determination not to be to obvious when his fans are around. Vince must see it because he gives Caleb a look when Chris drops his hand and pulls back.

"Wouldn't turn down Caleb the first time he actually invited me to something." Vince's tone isn't any better than Chris's. Caleb's just about to jump in and tell them to cool it when Danielle pushes between Chris and Vince. Caleb kind of loves her.

"Why're we all standing around? There's a table at the front. We're going to end up standing if you guys just keep standing around."

Danielle introduces herself to Vince and Marissa as they walk. At the table, she launches into a conversation about modeling with Marissa.

"You have to hang out with us after Vince goes back to New York," Danielle says. "There are way too many guys in our group and Jason's girlfriend hasn't moved out here yet. I'm outnumbered."

Marissa laughs and nods. "Sure. I don't know enough people since I moved here anyway."

"If they start plotting against us, I'm blaming you," Scott says, trying to laugh and ignore the way Chris is still trying to intimidate

Vince with the looks he's sending across the table. It's going to be a long night.

ഇൗൽ

"I WAS nice," Chris says when he climbs in the passenger seat of Caleb's SUV.

"You were glaring."

"*He* was glaring!"

"He was glaring because you were glaring." Caleb looks to Scott for help, but Scott just sighs and shakes his head.

Chris starts to say something else, but Scott reaches over from the backseat and lets his hand settle on the back of Chris's neck. Chris sighs and falls quiet.

"You can both try harder," Scott says. "Leave me sleeping alone again tonight, and you're both going to be making it up to *me*."

Caleb's not sure Scott believes their mumbled apologies, but he sits back and leaves them in silence the rest of the trip.

When they pull up in Jason's driveway, Caleb's almost surprised that Marissa's car pulls in after them. Then again, Marissa did hit it off with Danielle, and she hit Vince every time he looked like he was going to call Chris on being an asshole.

When Chris leaves to get Caleb a drink, Vince follows. Caleb starts after him, but both Marissa and Scott grab his arms to stop him.

"Let them hash it out," Scott says. "Chris knows better than to start a fight, and it's just going to be like this all night if you don't let it happen."

"And Vince knows my limits," Marissa says. "He's just worried about you, and he was too drunk to remember how Chris was with you when he picked you up."

"If this goes to hell, I'm blaming you both," Caleb answers, leaning into the arm Scott slips around his waist as Scott leads him to the couch.

Twenty minutes later, when Chris finally comes back with the drink Caleb's been wishing for, Chris pulls Caleb close to him on the couch and says, "I guess he's all right."

CHAPTER 24

"YOU'RE not supposed to be awake yet," Scott says when Caleb wakes up on the twentieth of December.

"We need to go to the airport." Both he and Chris have to be on a plane to Texas at eleven.

"We've got an hour. I was going to give you half an hour more." Scott scoots closer to him on the bed, draping his arm across Caleb's chest on top of Chris's.

"Why don't you go with Chris?" Caleb asks. Chris's mom knows Scott and Chris are together and she likes Scott. If Scott goes, then they'll both only be an hour and a half away instead of Chris being an hour and half and Scott being half-way across the country.

"Christmas is big for my family. Chris and I alternate Thanksgivings sometimes, but we don't usually do Christmas together. Our moms get too upset.

"So next year, you're going to Chris's for Thanksgiving?"

"It depends." Scott presses a kiss to his shoulder. "We're not leaving you alone if we can't bring you if that's what you're asking. We'll work something out by next year."

"I could go home, and we wouldn't be that far."

"We'll think about it. Next year. This year, you can make it ten days without me." Scott smiles as Chris shifts, snuggling against Caleb's side before he finally opens his eyes.

"Is it time to get up?" he mumbles into Caleb's neck.

"You can have fifteen minutes if you want it." Scott chuckles when Chris groans and flips over on his back.

"I'm already awake. Y'all owe me something for waking me up."

"We could do presents now." Scott says. He reaches over the side of the bed and comes back with two small boxes.

"We agreed to take the presents with us and open them on Christmas."

"Because you're too chicken to do it face to face. I want to do mine now."

"Scott's mom still has to hide his presents so he doesn't unwrap them and rewrap them before Christmas." Chris says, but he sits up and picks his up from the other side of the bed like they planned this and didn't tell him.

"It's not fair that I have to get up." Caleb frowns at Scott until he laughs and gets up to get the two slim envelopes Caleb left under the tree.

"Who's first?" Chris asks.

"I'm going last." Scott snatches away the two boxes before Chris and Caleb can stop him. It's not fair that he's already awake and they're still drowsy.

"Well I'm not going first." Chris says.

"Whatever. We said nothing big, right?" Caleb hands them each an envelope. "They're sort of different. You don't usually want the same thing."

Chris laughs as he pulls his booklet out of the envelope. "Sex however I want? You know I'm going to take you up on every single one of these, right?"

"I can't promise Scott's cooperation."

"I'll make a deal to follow his if he follows mine," Scott smiles as he flips though his own book of coupons.

"As long as it doesn't say 'fucking Chris like a girl' in there."

"Very romantic." Scott rolls his eyes at Chris, but he kisses Caleb. "Chris is next. I want my present."

"Here. You can open it." Chris waits until they unwrap two burned CDs before he finishes. "But you still can't listen until I'm gone. No listening on the plane while I'm sitting next to you either."

"You realize we know this is a love song now, right?" Scott leans over Caleb to kiss him, and Caleb breaks in. If Chris can write him a love song, he can give Chris the three-way kiss he's crazy about. Scott pulls away first, watching them finish the kiss before handing over the last of the gifts. Only now he has a matching box of his own.

"You bought yourself a present? I think we need to explain Christmas to you again," Caleb says as he tears away the paper on his.

"Just open it." Scott watches as they both pull off the box lids to reveal matching bracelets. Each bracelet is made of two strands of black leather braided with a thick silver wire.

"We said no big presents," Caleb says as Scott takes out his own bracelet.

"And I ignored you." Scott smiles and takes Caleb's bracelet to put it on his wrist. "Chris and I used to have different ones, but he broke them last time we broke up."

"I had both of them to break because Scott threw his at me." Chris says, but he's smiling as he takes Scott's bracelet to put it on before handing his own bracelet to Caleb and holding out his wrist.

"If you break this one, I'm kicking your ass."

"I promise not to break them if you promise not to throw them at me."

☯☪

CALEB wakes up in Dallas with his head on Chris's chest and Chris's arm around his shoulders.

"We're here." Chris leans down to kiss his forehead as the seat-belt light goes off.

"Did you call Scott?"

"Yeah, I told him you were drooling on my shirt. He says call him when you get back to your parents' house." Chris follows him down the aisle, leaving his hand on Caleb's hip as they walk.

Chris steps away when they get off the plane, but he nods toward the second bathroom they pass before they go back through security.

"I'll drive to you after Christmas, okay?" Chris says before wrapping his hand around the back of Caleb's head and pulling him close for kiss. The door opens and they break apart before they can get caught. In California, no one would blink twice, but they're back home in Texas now.

"Call me when you get home so I know you didn't die crossing into Oklahoma."

"Yeah." Chris looks around and sneaks another kiss before he turns and leads the way back into the crowd.

Caleb's mom spots him first, and she runs over with his sister. Samantha hugs him and then pulls back to let her eyes run over Chris.

"Seriously, you must be the best friend in the world. I can't believe you haven't tried to steal him from Scott."

Chris smirks, but he just shakes his head and doesn't argue.

"Why are all the hot ones gay? I *need* a picture of Scott now."

"Samantha!" His mom sighs before moving to hug Chris. "I've heard so much about you. It's so much better knowing Caleb's not in LA by himself with no one to take care of him. I can't thank you enough for watching out for him."

Caleb groans, but Chris just smiles and nods. "It's no problem, ma'am."

She smiles, hugging Chris again. "We'll let you go find your family now, but you have to come down from Thackerville for dinner before you leave."

Chris nods, all southern charm as he agrees to come to dinner, and excuses himself to go find his family.

Samantha punches Caleb in the arm as soon as Chris is out of sight. "Seriously. I hate you just for having him around to look at."

ᏸᏸ

WHEN he sees Scott on his caller ID the morning after Christmas, Caleb smiles and sneaks off to his old room. Scott will probably add in Chris and Caleb can come up with an excuse to go hang out with Chris instead of sticking around the house. There's only so many times his mom can try to set him up with some nice boy she meets through someone at PFLAG.

Caleb barely gets to say hello before Scott says, "Hold on. I already have Chris on the other line."

What's not normal is that Chris doesn't say anything when Scott pulls him into the call.

"Chris. You there?" Scott asks.

"Yeah." Chris doesn't sound right. His voice is weaker, rougher than it's supposed to be.

"Chris?" Caleb asks at the same time Scott says, "We have a problem, can you get away and come to Thackerville?"

"Yeah, sure. Now?" Caleb finds his keys in the pocket of the jeans he wore the day before. He still has a key to his mom's car that he can probably borrow.

"Yeah. Now," Scott says while Chris stays silent.

"Give me a minute." He doesn't want to put the phone down, but he can't just run off with his mom's car. He finds her downstairs in the kitchen making lunch.

"Can I take the car? Chris needs help with something."

"Everything okay?" She turns to look at him and sighs when he doesn't answer. He's going to have to tell her the truth soon. "Go. Call if you're not coming back tonight."

"I'm on my way," Caleb says when he picks up the phone again, talking as he heads to the car. "What's wrong?"

"Chris's mom got it out of him."

"She's not okay? Chris, you're freaking me out. Say something." Caleb's already planning where he can get away with speeding.

"She's disappointed. She said she's disappointed. I'm at a motel." Chris takes a deep breath, like just that was too hard for him to say. It probably was. Chris writes songs for his mama more than anyone else.

"Do you have the address?" Caleb's never been happier his mom invested in a GPS.

Chris finds some motel stationary and rambles off the address.

"How bad is he?" Caleb asks Scott when Chris hangs up.

"He's been crying. He told me he wasn't, but he was."

℘℃

CHRIS opens the door before Caleb knocks and pulls him inside the motel room. Caleb wraps both arms around him and to his surprise, Chris just sighs and leans into him, letting Caleb stand there holding him and rubbing his back.

That's when Caleb notices Chris is holding the phone. Caleb takes it from him as he leads Chris to the bed. He's not surprised when the display tells him it's Scott.

"Hey. I'm here," Caleb says into the phone as Chris curls up against his side, wrapping his arm around Caleb's chest and hiding his face in Caleb's neck.

"I know he's bad. How bad?" Scott asks.

"I haven't really gotten him to talk yet." Caleb turns back to Chris and moves his hand to brush through Chris's hair. He doesn't even look like Chris when he's curled up against Caleb, holding on like he's going to lose him. "Chris? Come on. I know I'm not Scott, but just say something."

"She's disappointed in me. She's never said that." Chris's voice cracks and he turns his face into Caleb's neck just as a tear slips out of his eye. It's just wrong. Chris isn't supposed to cry. He's not supposed to lie in Caleb's arms trying not to shake. Screw talking. Caleb turns on his side so he can pull Chris closer.

"I can try to get on a flight. Do I need to come?" Scott asks.

204

"Yeah. Just get here." Caleb hands the phone back to Chris so Scott can say goodbye. When Chris hangs up, he sighs and sags against Caleb, barely moving until his phone rings half an hour later. Chris bites his lip as he reads the caller ID.

"It's my mama."

"You want me to go?" Caleb's sure he *doesn't* want to leave, but he has to ask.

Chris shakes his head, pressing closer as he pushes the button to answer. "Mama?"

Whatever his mom says, it makes Chris relax. "I'm at a motel. Caleb's here. Scott's trying to get a flight."

Chris's face pales and he groans. "You called Scott's *parents?* Mama, I'm twenty-eight."

Chris pushes him away when he can't help smiling, but at least he looks like Chris again. He doesn't have his trademark smirk when he hangs up, but he doesn't just curl back against Caleb either.

"My mama wants to meet you," he says, putting down the phone so he can lace their fingers together.

"Okay." It's not like he can say no even if the idea kind of makes him want to throw up. He's not stupid. If she was going to like him, Chris wouldn't have been crying.

"You don't have to."

"Yeah, yeah, I do."

ℰℭℜ

CHRIS'S mama doesn't hug him or even shake his hand. She just stares at him, looking him over before turning to Chris and pulling him into her arms.

205

"I'm sorry, baby. I love you. I love you no matter what. We'll figure this out," she says. Chris relaxes a little, but Caleb doesn't miss that she doesn't really say it's okay. She lets go and takes Chris's hand to lead him inside. Chris looks back at him and nods his head for Caleb to follow.

She lets go of Chris in the living room and sits on the loveseat while Chris takes the couch. When he stands next to the couch like a dog waiting for permission, Chris turns to look at him. He doesn't say anything but he nods to the empty spot on the couch. Caleb sits next to him and Chris's mom just stares at him before looking away and focusing on Chris again.

"Baby, you have to understand why I can't just accept this," she says. Chris's hand reaches out, brushing against Caleb's, but he stops and brings it back to his lap. "I know you and Scott have had problems. I understand that, but if something isn't right, you can't just bring someone else in."

"Why not? If it's working, then why not?" Chris's voice is soft, unsure, but he reaches out and takes Caleb's hand, holding on and pulling Caleb's hand into his lap.

"Because that's not how it works. If you're having problems with Scott and you like someone else, you can't just have everything. You need to decide what you want."

"This is what I want." Chris sighs and his hand grips Caleb's harder. "This is what we all want. I'm not pushing Scott into this. Scott wanted it."

"That's what he said. I talked to him."

"You talked to Scott?" Chris turns to catch his eye for just a second.

"He called." She doesn't offer anything else. Caleb's going to kill Scott later for not warning them.

"Then he told you we both wanted this."

"He did. Baby, I know you wouldn't do something like this if you didn't think he wanted it too." She sighs, and Caleb catches her glancing to where Chris has his hand in a death grip. "But you can't deal with your problems like that. If you were fighting—"

"We weren't fighting," Chris interrupts. He bites his lip when she gives him a look. "Sorry, but we weren't. We were okay, but we both wanted this and we talked about it a lot. We really did. I know it's different, but we're happy."

She turns to Caleb for the first time. "And this is what you were looking for? You wanted to go into the middle of a relationship?"

Caleb freezes. It's like he's at a police station and everything he says will be held against him. Chris turns toward him and squeezes his hand. "It's okay."

"I wasn't looking for it. How could I be looking for it? But it's what I want." He knows his voice is shaking and that probably doesn't help, but Chris doesn't let go of his hand.

"And you're not doing this because you couldn't just have the one you wanted?" she asks, glancing from him to Chris. Chris tenses and starts to release his hand.

"No. I'm not." Caleb grips Chris's hand before he can let go and turns to face him. She's not the one that matters now. He's not stupid. He knows everyone thought he was just interested in Scott in the beginning. "I want *both* of you. I'm not in this because I couldn't just have Scott *or* just have you."

"I know." Chris lets out the breath he was holding. "I know."

She's silent until they turn back to her, but he can't tell by the look on her face if she believes them or not.

"Scott said he's trying to get a flight tonight," she finally says. "You should stay tonight. I want to talk to all of you when he gets there. I'll fix up the guestroom."

"The guestroom?" Chris asks. "We're back to the guestroom?"

"I just met him. I just found out about this. I need time." She gets up, ending the conversation there.

"I'm sorry," Chris says after she leaves the room. "You don't have to. You can meet us in Dallas tomorrow, or you can sleep with me. She'll get over it if I insist."

"It's okay." This is already bad enough. She's going to hate him even more if he makes a fuss and he doesn't want to leave Chris by himself, either.

"Okay." Chris sighs, glances in the direction his mom left to, and then kisses him. "I'll call Scott first and then tell him to call you?"

"Yeah, sure." Caleb nods, standing when Chris's mama comes back in the room.

"I'll see you in the morning." She hugs Chris and kisses his cheek before nodding to him and leaving down the hall.

Chris walks him to the guestroom and stops just inside the door. He tries to remember how much it freaked him out when Scott's parents put them all in the same room at Thanksgiving, but that was just awkward. It's worse when he's not even sure what's going to happen after Scott gets there. If Chris's mama can't get behind him, he's not sure how it's going to work. Chris is closer to his mama than anyone else he's ever dated.

"Hey." Chris lifts his chin and kisses him again. "I'll see you in the morning. Scott'll get here and it'll be fine."

Chris turns to go, then stops, and spins around to come back. He glances down the hall to his mama's room before pulling his T-shirt over his head. He pushes it into Caleb's hands before kissing him again and disappearing into his room.

It's weird sitting in the room without Chris. He calls his mom and avoids her worried questions when he tells her he's staying over. Then he just has to wait for Scott's call. All week he's hated sleeping alone, but at least he had both of them on the phone, sometimes until he fell asleep. Now he just has Chris's shirt and an empty bed.

At least the night before he could count the days until he was with them again. Now he's not sure they'll even be together at New Year's.

Because he can't be the reason Chris can't talk to his mama. It's bad enough that his dad left a long time ago. He can't be the reason Chris doesn't have family. And if she makes Chris pick, he can't be the reason Chris and Scott aren't together. Chris and Scott belong together and it's not like he could really pick between them.

He's already decided what he has to say when Scott calls.

"Hey, I heard it was bad. Chris is worried about you." Scott's voice is soft and it's not fair that he's all the way across the country.

"I'm okay," he lies.

"I would've called to tell you I talked to her, but I thought I was going to get on a flight. I should be able to get on a red-eye though. I'll be there by morning."

"Okay."

"Babe, are you okay? Really? You don't sound okay."

"If you have to, I want you to pick Chris," Caleb says before he can chicken out.

"What? Caleb, it's not that bad. That's not happening."

"It might. If it comes to it, I want you to pick Chris. Just say you'll do it." There's a lump in his throat, but he's pretty sure he still sounds confident.

"No. I'm not saying that. This isn't about me and Chris. It hasn't been for a long time. I'm not picking because that's not going to happen. Chris isn't going to let that happen. Chris loves you. *I* love you."

"You don't know it's not going to happen."

"Yes. I do know," Scott says, but he wasn't there. He didn't see how she only looked at Caleb once. "I just got off the phone with Chris. He says it's going to be rough, but she'll see that we all want this and she'll get over it. He thinks you're mostly okay."

"She's not going to get over it. She didn't even want to look at me."

"Baby." Scott's pleading is enough to make him crack. The tears slip out and he knows Scott can hear that he's crying when he says, "Go to Chris. Go to him and let him tell you it's gonna be okay."

"I can't. She already hates me. She'll hate me more if I break her rules."

"Yes, you can. Hell, if Chris knew you were crying, he'd be there." The sound of the airport announcements paging Scott Anderson comes over the line and he can hear Scott getting up. "Caleb, please. They're paging me for a flight, but you need to just go to him. She'll get over it."

"I can't," he says. He can hear Scott talking to someone about his flight.

"You can. Shit. Okay, I have to go and get this flight. Then I'm calling Chris and telling on you."

"Scott."

"I love you. Now I'm calling Chris." Scott hangs up. A few minutes later, Caleb hears the phone ringing through the wall, but it doesn't matter. Chris is in the shower and he probably won't check his messages.

CHAPTER 25

THE next morning, it doesn't look like Chris has slept at all. His eyelids are drooping as he catches Caleb coming out of the shower.

"Why do I have a message from Scott telling me to check on you? I didn't see it until this morning." Chris wraps his arms around Caleb's waist, pulling Caleb into his arms.

"It's nothing. Scott worries too much." Caleb lets himself relax in Chris's arms. He might as well if this is going to be one of the last times they're together.

"You sure? He sounded really worried." Chris pulls him back and kisses him, but Caleb doesn't let the kiss linger. The last thing he needs is Chris's mom coming around the corner and getting mad.

"I'm sure."

"Okay." Chris lets him go and moves around him to get to the bathroom. "I left a clean shirt on the bed for you. It's probably a little big, but I think I like how you look in my clothes anyway."

Chris disappears into the bathroom, leaving Caleb to hide in the guestroom until Chris knocks on his door and comes in.

"We gotta go get Scott. My mama's insisting on driving. That okay?"

"Sure." Caleb shrugs, letting Chris kiss him again, before Chris takes his hand and leads him out the door to where she's already waiting in her SUV. She glances at their joined hands, but she doesn't say anything when Chris climbs in the back, pulling Caleb in to sit next to him.

It's a quiet ride. Every few minutes, Chris's thumb rubs over the back of his hand, but neither he nor Chris dares to move much. When they get to the airport, Chris squeezes his hand before letting go and shoving his hands in his pockets for the walk to baggage claim. Scott's plane hasn't landed yet, leaving them to sit in awkward silence until the screen finally blinks to ARRIVED.

Chris sees Scott first. He taps Caleb and points before getting up. He doesn't even pretend not to be relieved. He just hurries toward Scott and into his arms. Scott says something Caleb can't hear and they turn, moving back to where he's standing next to Chris's mom.

Scott hugs him, holding him while Chris combs fingers through his hair.

"It's okay. It's all gonna be fine," Scott says before letting him go and turning to hug Chris's mama. She hugs Scott back even though she's still barely even looked at Caleb.

Scott sits in between them on the way back, holding their hands together in his lap and refusing to let go even when Chris's mom looks at him. Her lips form one hard line, but she turns back to the road without comment.

At the house, Scott refuses to let them go even when they go through the door. Chris gives them a look, but Scott just sighs and mouths *later*.

"You seem as determined as my son," Chris's mom says as soon as they sit down in the living room. Scott sits between them on the couch, still holding Caleb's hand and leaving his other hand on Chris's thigh.

"We know what we want. We talked about it a lot, more than we've ever talked about anything, and we both agreed and then we talked about it with Caleb. We didn't just see him in a bar one day and decide we wanted a new boyfriend."

"So how did you meet him?" She glances back to their joined hands.

"Jason introduced us." At least Scott leaves out how Jason met him. "We'd been hanging out with him a few months before anything happened, but it just got more and more obvious that we were both falling for him. We couldn't hide it from each other and we had to deal with it."

"And this is how you decided to deal with it? You never thought that maybe you should break up if you wanted someone else."

"I love Chris," Scott says.

"And I love Scott. We didn't want to break up," Chris adds. "We both wanted the same thing and we were okay with trying this, so we brought it up to Caleb."

"I can't for the life of me figure out why he'd agree to that." She sighs and combs a hand through her short hair. "It's not fair for him either."

Chris looks at him, like he's also not sure why Caleb accepted the offer. Scott's thumb rubs over the back of his hand as they all turn to him.

"I didn't want to break them up, and I wanted, cared about, both of them." Caleb glances at Chris, who smiles a little and gives him a nod. "I never expected this to happen, but I love them. I couldn't pick between them if they asked me."

"We wouldn't." Chris bites his lip and waits for Scott to nod before he finishes. "And we're not going to pick each other and leave him either. I love him and Scott loves him, and we're happy with that. Mama, we're happy. I just want you to be happy that I'm happy."

"Chris, baby." She sighs again, but she gets up and sits next to Chris on the only empty space on the couch. "I just don't see how this can work long-term. Something's going to happen, and someone is going to want to pick."

"You don't know that. None of us want things to change. We're *happy*, mama. Happier than before. Scott and I haven't even really fought in months. We're stronger like this. It's like how triangles are used in building supports because they're the strongest shape."

"You aren't a building support," she says. Caleb kind of has to agree with her on that one.

"Okay, not the best example, but Mama, this *works* for us." Chris sounds so confident, Caleb might believe it if he didn't see the way Chris is gripping Scott's thigh.

"And there's no changing your mind?"

"Someone once told me that if I loved someone, nothing could talk me into leaving them. Not even my mama."

She finally smiles, picks up Chris's hand and kisses the top of it. "You know, you're not supposed to use my own words against me."

"You were right."

"Then I guess I have to get used it. I'll try, but baby, you can't expect me to get used to this right away."

"I just want you to give it a chance, Mama." Chris pulls away from Scott to hug her and she holds on for a long time before getting up.

"I should make lunch. I'm sure you boys are hungry. Caleb, you're welcome to stay." She makes it less of an invitation and more of an order, but it's better than getting thrown out the door. Still, the whole thing is a sudden jump.

"She cooks when she's upset," Chris says.

"I'm sorry."

"Not your fault, darlin'. She'll get over it. She got over me dating guys in high school. She'll get over this."

Caleb's not so sure, but Scott pulls Chris close and kisses him. "She will. She loves you."

"Yeah." Chris sighs and sags against Scott for a few seconds before he sits up and says, "You wanna tell me what's going on now?"

"It's probably going to have to wait until tonight." Scott nods to the kitchen.

Chris nods his agreement, but he gives Caleb a worried glance. "If she still doesn't want us all together, you two are both in the guestroom. Putting Scott with me isn't going to help."

"Yeah," Scott agrees, but he adds, "Try to get all of us in your room?"

℘つ℃

LUNCH is awkward. Dinner is worse, but when Caleb suggests heading home, Chris's mama gives him a glare and says, "Chris doesn't need to be with anyone I haven't gotten to know."

Caleb's coming out from a shower when he almost walks in on Chris talking to his mom in the living room.

"We talked about it. Scott's staying with Caleb. That's gonna have to work unless you're gonna put Scott out on the couch."

"This is my house," she says.

215

"And if you have any issues with people sharing beds, it should be with them sharing with me."

"You have to know this is difficult for me." She sighs, pushing her hair back from her face.

"And it's difficult for us too. You think this is easy for them? I don't want either of them alone, so you leave me alone, or you let them come to my room." Chris sighs and sits down on the couch. "Mama, please try. We need some time. You've been at us all day. Give us some time."

"You will behave yourselves." She fixes her eyes on Chris until he nods, as if they'd do anything with her in the house anyway.

She hugs Chris, kisses his cheek, and Caleb steps back in the bathroom before she can catch him spying on her way to bed. There's a knock on the door a second later.

"I saw you eavesdropping," Chris says through the door.

"I didn't mean to." Caleb opens the door, and steps into Chris's arms.

"Come on. Scott's already moving your stuff." Chris leads him down the hall to and pulls him into the room where Scott is already stripping off his shirt. Scott's silent as he gets rid of the T-shirt Caleb threw on after his shower and pulls back the sheets.

"Y'all ready to tell me what the hell's going on that I don't know about?" Chris asks, pulling Caleb into bed after him.

"Nothing's going on." Caleb says, turning on his side away from Chris.

"That why you won't look at me?"

"We always sleep like this." It's true. Nine out of ten nights, he falls asleep facing Scott with Chris spooned close behind him.

"Maybe, but Scott's gonna tell me the truth anyway." Chris tries to get him to turn over on his back, but Caleb ignores him. This isn't how they do things. Scott should just be telling Chris later.

"No. Caleb's gonna tell you himself." Scott catches him off guard and pushes him on his back.

"Why're we doing this? This isn't how we do shit."

"Because you should've done it last night instead of telling Chris you were okay."

"You weren't okay?" Chris props himself up on his elbow to watch Caleb's face. "Darlin', if you weren't okay, why didn't you say something?"

"You had other things to worry about."

Scott presses closer, snuggling against him until Caleb turns on his side, not realizing until Scott's spooned behind him that now he's trapped into facing Chris.

"You still should've told me." Chris sighs, looking down. "I told you when I wasn't okay. I mean, yeah, I called Scott first, but he pointed out that you were closer and I wanted him to call you. Should I have just waited until Scott could get on a flight?"

"No."

"So why'd you think you couldn't come to me? Maybe we suck at talking, but I could've been with you." Chris's fingers trace over his chest, but Caleb still isn't looking at him. "Unless you didn't want me. Unless you just wanted Scott."

"No." Shit. Now he's really fucking things up. "I just didn't want to make your mom more mad than she already was."

"You gonna tell me what you were upset about now? Was it just my mama? Because I know she seems tough, but she'll end up okay."

217

It's on the tip of his tongue to say that's all it was, but Scott whispers in his ear, "Don't try it. Tell him what you were thinking."

"Why?"

"Because I should've told him what you were thinking when my parents found out. I should have told him how much you worried instead of just trying to deal with it myself, and you should know better than think you can't talk to him when I'm not there."

Chris looks over his shoulder at Scott. "You're supposed to tell me anything important."

"I know. I should've told you. But I tried to call you last night." Scott's arms tighten around Caleb.

"So someone tell me what I missed."

Caleb sighs, closing his eyes so he doesn't have to see Chris's reaction. "I just thought it'd be easier if it was just y'all."

"What?" Chris cups his cheek. "Is that what you want? Just because it might be easier?"

"No. Fuck, no. I just thought you might want to." Caleb stops. There's no point in adding *break up with me*.

"What? How could you even think that? Darlin', look at me." Chris sighs, takes a deep breath, and when Caleb opens his eyes, Chris is looking straight into them. "I love you. How could you think I'd want to just give you up?"

"I know. But your mom was so upset, and she was pressuring you to pick between us. I just, I wasn't sure you'd think it was worth it." Caleb pulls away. He can't look at Chris and not lose it.

"Fuck. Darlin', don't you ever think that. *Nothing* is going to make me pick between you. It's been a hell of a long time since we could pick each other over you. We figured it out the first time you left for New York, and we talked about it." Chris reaches for him, pulling him close and holding him tight until he takes a deep breath and cracks, letting a few tears out.

"No one told me you talked about it." He's not sure it would have worked this time, but it might have helped when Scott's parents found out.

"We thought you knew," Chris whispers, wiping the tears away with his thumb. "Next time, you get me. I don't give a shit if it's complicated or it'll piss someone off. If you're upset, you come get me."

Caleb nods, sighing and relaxing between them. Chris kisses his lips and his forehead as his hands stroke over Caleb's back.

When he's calmed down, Scott lets him go and props himself up on his elbows so Caleb and Chris can both see him.

"See? You talked to each other, and the world didn't end."

EPILOGUE

"IF YOU guys don't show up, we're going to assume you're having an orgy," Danielle says at Scott's show when they get back to California. Only Scott would do a show the day before New Year's Eve, but at least it's an excuse to see everyone on the thirtieth so they can spend New Year's Eve alone. At least that was the plan. Everyone else is still trying to convince them to go to Jason's New Years Eve party.

"Is what they do really an orgy? Or do you mean like an orgy with extra people? Because I don't think Chris would do that," Marissa says, cocking her head at Caleb. It occurs to Caleb that instead of just worrying about Vince, he should have worried about introducing Marissa to Danielle.

"He wouldn't. I tried to get in on it before and they said no," Danielle says.

"So we're back to deciding if what they do is an orgy?" Marissa turns to Vince who shakes his head.

"There is a limit to how much I want to think about it."

"Whatever," Danielle pushes back a loose strand of red hair. "The point is that if you don't come to my party, we're going to assume you guys are having an orgy."

Caleb figures he probably shouldn't point out that the reason he doesn't want to go is so they can spend the night in bed. He thought they were going to break up with him. He deserves a night in bed. Actually, he was planning for a whole day.

"If we agree to go, will you drop the orgy thing before Caleb refuses to have sex with me ever again?" Chris says, laughing when Caleb slaps his arm.

"For a few days," Danielle says.

"Three weeks," Chris counters.

"Two weeks."

"Fine." They shake on it.

Chris leans close, lips brushing against his ear as he whispers, "We'll just stay sober enough to go home and fuck after. I promise we'll stay in bed the next day."

℘CR

IT'S two minutes until midnight, and Caleb's still not sure he's going to get a kiss when the ball drops. He's sure he'll get a kiss sometime around midnight, but he'd rather have one right as the clock strikes twelve. It's stupid and it's probably the dumbest superstition he has, but everyone still does it and it's not fair that he doesn't know how it's going to work for them.

Because they've never done the whole three-way kiss in front of people. During sex, or leading to sex, of course, but Chris never tries it in front of other people, and Chris is always the one who starts it. So this can only mean that Chris doesn't want to do it in front of other people.

Usually Caleb's fine with that. He likes that Chris likes to keep some things behind closed doors. Not everything needs to be public information. Especially considering how much Danielle dwells on everything that is, which is why Caleb wanted to spend New Year's Eve at Scott's house without other people. Now they'll probably take turns, and even if they kiss him before they kiss each other, it won't be the same.

"Hey. We were looking for you." Scott moves to stand next him, dragging Chris behind him. "Well, I was looking for you. Chris was making jokes about balls dropping. One of us is going to have to drive home because he's had enough to drink already."

"I'm not drunk. It's just funny." Chris moves closer to Caleb, wrapping his arm around Caleb's waist and kissing his neck. "It was not enough to threaten to ditch me for the countdown."

"You knew I was joking." Scott laughs as the countdown starts on Danielle's TV. He steps closer, filling in the empty space in their triangle.

"You owe me. I hid Danielle's camera." Chris smirks, before wrapping a hand behind each of their necks to pull them both into one kiss as the countdown ends. Caleb's sure he sees the flash of a camera anyway, but he'll worry about stealing the camera later.

TESSA CÁRDENAS grew up in a small town in northern Texas before relocating to Florida to study creative writing. Since completing her degree, she spends her days educating young minds and wouldn't quit her day job even if she could. She's traveled to Europe, Asia, and all over the United States and Canada, but she'll always be a Texas girl. She currently lives with two dogs, one cat, and a stack of works in progress.